Women Dancing in Pine Valley

Camilla Danilda

Translation Lisza Ray

Woman dancing
in pine valley

Camilla Danilda

Swedish
Author

It`s time to live our unique expressions
like mothers, sisters, and in relation to
men!

Susanna Billander, multi-dimesional
catalyst, who guides people to activate
their abundant expression of love in their
relationships.

Original titel: Dansa med livet
© 2018 Camilla Danilda
Print in Baltic JSC Litauen
Front cover: www.ethosdesign.se
Front cover modell: Yessica Diana
Translation: Lisza Ray
Design: Edita Ramoniene, Print in Baltic JSC
ISBN: 9789198110777
First edition

Who would I be if I started to dance with life?
If life in its whole was an expression of a complete woman.
If the imprint and the expression was a dream as much in
me as around me.
If this whole couldn't be separated:
Who am I then?

Ann

My love is by my side. We play. I feel so true. We walk on a beach. He holds my hand. We walk on yet another beach. His hand fits perfect in mine. There's sand between my toes. I look at his feet. His big toes are a bit askew. There's sand between the toes. He's got black hair on his feet. I look at my feet. They have pink nail polish. We walk. Sometimes we stop. "Look", I say, "a crab". He doesn't see it. He cannot hear me. The wind catches my hair. He points at a big cliff. We walk towards it. I look at the hair on his foot. They move in the wind. We climb a steep cliff. The sea laps beneath us. We are safe. I'm safe. The wind blows. He reaches out. We get to the top. He pulls me into his arms. Smiles at me. We stand in each other's arms. Time doesn't exist. I know that I have experienced this before. I recognize it. I feel whole. I smell something strange. The ocean. Something is rotten. The wind increases. A wild, loud noise. A train comes rushing along. It separates me from him. Splits us in two. I'm thrown back. I fall. Someone calls out. Separation. I can't hear. I don't want to hear. I have no ears. I fall.

Ann wakes up abruptly. Her eyes open. She doesn't move, just lies perfectly still. She's still falling but is at the same time aware of a bed and an unsuccessfully drilled whole in the ceiling. It's askew. The sound of the train cuts deafening in her. The anxiety cuts like knifes, stings alarmingly under her skin. The abyss is inevitable. The night hours are to few. Her body aches. The dreams come with the sleep. A feeling of powerless fear. The feeling of not knowing where she is when she wakes up. Or who she is. For just a few seconds she thinks she wakes up in the so familiar bedroom at Winding Road. Next to her, Samuel lies on his back. His hair is wet on his forehead and the quilt lies diagonally over them. She can see a part of those brightly coloured underwear she always buys him for Christmas. She looks out through the door to the terrace that leads to the perfectly sized garden. The pelargoniums and a rose geranium are in bloom in the window. She's had them for over twenty years. The walls are filled with framed paintings their children painted when they were small. A happy cephalopod in bright colours. A rainbow and a heart with the word 'Mom' written in it. An ordinary day in an ordinary life. She tries to close her eyes. But the dream becomes clear: it was the two of them again. On a journey. They walked hand in hand. The feeling of safety and love was their point of attachment. They were one. Her life's purpose was fulfilled. A couple. He held her, there at the edge of the cliff. The train had thrown her off the cliff. She falls ... She's alone, not missed. The other side of the double bed is untouched.

10

She sighs and puts her legs over the bedside. Dizziness. Sits for a while before logic catches up. Her mouth is dry and her lips are chapped. The glass on the bedside table is empty. The lip salve has rolled onto the floor. Dust balls and piles of clothes are playing in the faint sunlight. She doesn't have the strength to bother today, either, but gets up as a routine and goes into the bathroom. Her glance freezes in the mirror. She tries to put on a stiff smile. She feels just as vague as she looks. The sleep at night wears her out. Flakes of skin are peeling off her forehead and more rashes has appeared. She should drink more water. Why doesn't she eat regularly? Start exercising again? She turns around, her behind looks flat and loose in the mirror. She studies her body with critical eyes. Has she stopped caring? The children have taught her to love in another way. They are now grown-up and she's getting on towards fifty. She beats herself verbally, looks with contempt at the fat woman she sees in the mirror. She knows that the separation has nothing to do with her not being good enough, not being pretty enough. But all logic disappeared when the feelings took over. They made her feel insecure and indifferent. The confusion grew in a constant mix of thoughts and feelings. Between now and then.

She sighed again and stepped into the shower. She wished that she was someone else today. That she could get her old life back. But was that really what she wanted? She didn't know anymore. There was a security in the old routines that disguised her as self-evident. A part she played, she was someone! She had always been his.

She had thought that Samuel had made a joke when the words had left his lips: "I want a divorce!" The palpitations had come creeping up on her. A sudden tsunami that took what she had loved:

The family.

The children.

The years.

She wasn't prepared for the fact that he would be unreasonable. Fight over the house, the money and the children. That had made her passive. Made her move to an apartment, give up instead of making adult choices. In her experience, fighting and arguing didn't help. How many clients hadn't she guided through their divorces? How many times in her role as a therapist and expert on couples' therapy? She didn't know. She had never really understood there could be a physical effect, that it could be felt under the skin. She'd never understood that painful words would find their way into the deepest corners and destroy shared memories. While she covered her body with soap, she realized she no longer knew who she was. It was like walking in newly-fallen snow. To walk where no feet had ever walked before.

1986

She was raring to go. The party mood was bubbling in her body. The hairstyling gel was sticky on her hands when she squeezed it into her curls. Fixed the fringe. The bottle of hairspray was almost empty, but she shook it with the beat from the music playing on the tape recorder. The ball rolled inside. She was careful not to get foundation on her new white blouse with ruffles. Green eyeshadow sparkled over the blue mascara. Her hair swung in time with the music that was booming out from the speaker. She scrutinized herself in the mirrored wall. She was satisfied with the new black fishnets to the short black leather skirt. She put the make-up in her handbag. Put on the fake leather waist-length jacket and slipped out without saying goodbye. In the background, she could hear the clinking glasses and the loud voices in the living room. The New Year's Eve was awaiting. It was cold outside. The bottles of spirits were clinking in her handbag. The bus driver's glance moved to her fishnet tights. Shit, what a dirty old man, she thought but felt proud at the same time. Today, she felt as if she was at least eighteen. This would be a great night.

She froze in her short jacket, which crackled in the cold. For a moment, she wished she had both a woolly hat and a pair of mittens. The long, backcombed hair straggled and glistened of snow crystals. She passed several houses with flickering outdoor candles before she could hear the loud pulsating music from the terraced house. For a second, she thought of ringing the doorbell, but who would hear her?

The hall was crowded with people and she tripped over shoes and boots. She took off her high-heeled boots but changed her mind and slid them on again. She was shivering from the cold after the short walk from the bus. She made her way through the crowd and looked into the living room to see if there was anyone she knew. She continued into the kitchen, it seemed to be just as crowded. With perfect ease she picked up a glass from the table.

”But hello there, don't I know you?”

She looked into a pair of blue eyes. No, not that she could remember.

”I don't think so!”

”Chris, for fuck's sake. You should know that you can't always use that line”, a guy by the window yelled.

”Don't mind them, they are really drunk”, said the guy with the blue eyes.

Chris was a couple of years older. With a deft hand he poured her a glass with something that looked like lemonade and brought her into the living room. Someone had lit a cigarette. The music was booming from the big speakers in each corner. It was so loud you couldn't hear your own thoughts.

"Would you like to dance?"

She nodded in response, tried to smile. She could dance. She had dreamt of being a professional dancer when she was younger, but there had never been any money for dance classes.

He leaned in again. "I hate to dance, but I'd love to dance with you!" She smiled, embarrassed, and hoped he wouldn't see that she was blushing. Chris handed her the glass. The liquid scorched her throat when she knocked it back.

"Good girl!"

The affects of the drink made her shyness turn into a more comforting feeling. Chris got them more drinks and she accepted them thankfully. They were so easy to drink. Chris didn't take his eyes off her. She danced. She wished that they were going out together. She had never had a real boyfriend. Not an older one. A slow song started and Chris pulled her into his arms to dance cheek-to-cheek. His hand travelled up and down her back. Then, he took her upstairs. Everything was rocking when she walked, but he made her feel so happy. He fiddled with a door for a while before they got into a bedroom. He pulled up a cigarette he had rolled himself. It was glowing in the dark, the music downstairs felt distant. She felt very tired now.

***

The ice floes were all over the place. Some of them had tipped over and reminded her of ice-cream cones and made her feel even colder. Cold, stinging air pressed its way into her lungs. She leaned over the rail. Deep down under the ice she could vaguely make out there was a precipice. A darkness far from the stress of the surrounding world. The darkness appealed to her, deep below the surface. Far from this moment. The thought of letting her body slide unnoticed under the ice was tempting. She imagined how the cold water surrounded her, took over her body. The further down towards the bottom she sank, the more her skin dissolved – and with that, the ability to feel. There were no more bounds. Memories were erased. Her longing to let the icy water embrace her last breath scared her. That yearning hadn't been there yesterday! It had emerged during the night between 1986 and 1987. A hole in the ice, and they would find her in springtime. All swollen and unrecognizable. It was there, the comfort in knowing there was an end.

No feelings.

No words.

Only an end.

Her fingers squeezed the rail, as if they tried to keep her alive. She looked anxiously over her shoulder. Someone was there, she knew that. She looked up into the sky, as if it would tell her that. But the sky was waiting with its answers

16

and the same haze appeared to cover all of Greenville. With a heavy sigh she was forced to continue by the cold. The ice wouldn't welcome her last breath today and her legs staggered on by themselves, even though the thought was tempting. The high heels made her walk with a stoop. It was difficult to tell the hours apart from one another. How had she gotten from one place to here? Everything in between was a haze. Incoherent fragments. Loose ends. A word here, a word there, and one that echoed in the the obscure background.

All she wanted was to forget. To sink down to a bottomless abyss. She would forget! Wouldn't tell anyone. It would remain a silent secret. She would continue living as if it had never happened. She started to fantasize about the warmth. A shower and a warm bed. She turned towards the subway. A faint smell of vomit and fireworks gave evidence of the New Year's Eve.

Nothing else.

Silent.

Quiet.

Down at the platform she once again got the feeling that someone else was there. Was she being followed? She swung around but there was only emptiness. She walked apathetically back and forth to get warmer. She hardly heard the screech from the brakes when the train slowed down. Nor did she smell the stench of vomit that met her when the doors opened. Yet, instinctively, she stayed by the doors prepared to change carriage at the next stop. She looked at her reflection in the doors. Was that the same girl that only twelve hours ago had been laughing? Pictures of yesterday flashed by – she danced. That cute guy had offered her drinks. And that cigarette that had tasted different. It had made her loose-limp, yet pleasantly relaxed. He had encouraged her. She had surrendered to him. He'd made her do things she'd never done before.

It was as if she was covered with a film of death. The same musty smell that spread in the train carriage. She felt sick now. She wet her forefinger with her tongue and tried unsuccessfully to wipe away some thinly spread out blue mascara under her eyes. Yesterday, she had spent so much time in front of the mirror. She had felt so sure, had known that she was doing the right thing. The green eyeshadow to match her eyes. Black eyeliner. The white blouse with its ruffles, a new bra and the neat waist-length jacket. Wasn't that also what he'd said? That she looked hot? She touched her neck. Love bites. The necklace she'd got from her grandmother as a gift on her confirmation day was gone. She tried to pull up the jacket, even though it didn't have a collar. She inspected her hair, it was still backcombed. She couldn't remember. Everything was shrouded in a mist. She didn't understand how it all connected. Just fragments and loose ends that could never be organized. There was a before and an after, but the in-between was gone. Someone had said something! A few words that had stuck to her, that was all. The subway train finally slowed down. Out of habit she looked for her purse but couldn't find it. Hadn't she had one?

A shadow joined her, a hand over her mouth. Before she knew it, she was stuck in the grip. The last thing she felt was the cold that hit her bare skin under the fishnets.

"Not the slightest sound, or you'll die!"

***

The ashes on the table was spread like fruit flies. A couple of coffee stains had been smudged out when the ashtray had been moved around. It was full. The smoke made her feel sick.

"May I have a drag? Hello, Mum?"

"What? Yes, sure." The mother handed her cigarette to her daughter.

She got dizzy when she took a deep drag, the smoke curled its way out through her nose and mouth. The throat ached but it still gave her some comfort. The last twenty-four hours reality reminded her of a life with dizziness, feeling of sickness and that nasty lump that grew in her stomach. She had no idea how she should handle the lump. She wanted to scream but couldn't.

"I have to go through this again. Am I boring you? It was so typical. Exactly at twelve, he turned away from me and kind of smiled at her. You have never met her, have you? She's not ugly, but it's like she's wrapped in a dirty film. She just looks so cheap! What does he see in her, I don't get it? And she has an ugly body. You get it? No breasts. Totally flat!" Her mother stroke with her hands over her own body to show how flat the woman's breasts were.

She looked at her. Her mother really looked terrible. The dressing gown needed a wash. She had old mascara under her eyes. The skin looked sallow, like a dirty window in the spring's sunshine. She had been crying. She reached for the pack of cigarettes and took one. Chain-smoking. That's what it was called when you smoked and smoked, created long chains. Chains that could not be torn away, that needed to be cured. The daughter stubbed it out in the ashtray. The cigarette smoke lay like a thick fog and for a moment she wished that she would dare to open the window. But the cold outside scared her. It had found its way inside of her, taken possession of her body. She wanted to tell her mother about the night. But where to begin? Every time she tried, the lump grew, and she felt like she needed to run to the toilet. But once she sat there, nothing came. It was as if it had never happened. That she had imagined it. She glanced at her mother. She didn't want to become a chain-smoker. No, she wouldn't get hooked. She wouldn't sit there and smoke and moan over men. Instead, she would give her time to her children. Ask them questions. Listen. Her mother never listened to her. She just smoked and was preoccupied with her own stuff, like whether or not David was the only man in the world. Always the same drama.

20

Why is it that she sits here, smoking and crying? She'll take him back anyway. As she did with Barry. He hit her black and blue, but she forgave him anyway. No, she would never be like her mother and let the men have that kind of power over her.

"I'll never be able to forgive him for this, just at the strike of twelve! Do you get that? On New Year's Eve! The whole year is ruined now!" Her mother gave a sob.

"But you will forgive him. You always do!"

"That's not fair!" Her mother indignantly wiped her tears on the sleeve of her dressing gown.

"No, all my life I've been listening to you nagging about your dirty men."

"But ..."

"There's no bloody but, do you get me? What about me? You never listen to me!"

"Sure I do!"

She braced her hands against the table and stood up so quickly that the chair fell over. On pure impulse she grabbed the ashtray and threw it into the refrigerator door. The anger spread in her and she searched for something more to throw. She wanted to grab her mother, give her a shake, hit her. She gave her mother a piercing look, as if it was a sharp object, and hissed the words:

"Don't you get it? Nobody wants to have a mother who's a fucking crack whore. Get a grip!"

She pushed the table towards her mother and ran into her room. The slam from the door made a diploma fall off the wall. The strong sobs surprised her. One word echoed speechlessly in her head. For every sob it dug deeper in. She felt unfairly treated, angry and sad at the same time.

She woke up in a cold sweat. What was it she'd been dreaming? Her body was aching, and it was hot in the room. She lay totally still and didn't dare to move. The dream lingered in the room like a thick fog. It was dark outside. It couldn't be past midnight. She tried to remember what had happened on New Year's Eve. Chris, who she'd never met before, had made her let loose on the dance floor. She'd been giggling hysterically, and he had made her feel free and easy. He had mumbled into her ear: "I hate to dance, but you make me want to do more." He had touched her. Surely he had? It was a gentle hand that touched her arm and once her back. As if she was someone special. Someone had been smoking weed in the kitchen. The party had been even more crowded. He had taken her hand. They had sat hand in hand and shared a cigarette he had rolled himself. After that, everything had become strange and dizzy. The next thing she knew, she'd been on her way home. Had he followed her? After that, everything had gone black.

The lump in her stomach grew. She turned her back to the door and pulled the cover over her head. She didn't want to know! When the day started dawning, she fell into a dreamless sleep.

The Dance of Origins

In the beginning there was nothing else but entirety. The sound, the smells and the universe were vibrating with harmonic tones. An impulse of constantly loving whirls that became visible by the all-seeing. In the land beyond the sun there's a planet that's richer than any other. Here, life is always present in the divine.

The glade in the forest is surrounded by majestic trees. Soft sun-rays shimmer down between the foliage and reflect in the light of the rainbow. In the land where the sun never sets there is no time. There is only the omniscient coloured by the stardust. Everything living is absorbed and spread by the waves of energy. Nothing is separated from the other. It is a loving game. The wing strokes of the butterflies affect the nectar to flow. Even in the soft tufts of grass, life is present. The spirit. Without separation from the universe. The delicate meadow flowers offer nutriment for everything and everyone.

A heavenly beautiful white angel shape moves freely in the glade. It is the movement itself that is the experience, not the goal. The sensations of the mind show her the way. The boundaries on this side of the sun are not as clear. Unconditionally the whole flows connected with natural bonds in freedom. She bends down and smells a violet. The fragrance of vanilla and its sweetness makes her skin vibrate as she senses a high, flute like tone. She closes her eyes to listen closely and when she opens them from this meditative state her senses are extra sharp. Her eyes see the colours in their true reflection in the shimmer from the rainbow. Her hearing is nothing but harmonic vibrant tones. It is as if the tree trunks a bit further call on her attention and she gets closer to them in dancing moves. Her naked feet absorb nutrients. A golden sap trickles from the tree. She gets closer to the trunk as if it is a beloved, patiently waiting for her. The tip of her tongue slowly drinks the sap. The body responds with a humming and the essence runs healing down her throat. She follows it in her mind, like a glowing path all the way down to her stomach, where it explosively gives her new power. All of a sudden, she knows where to go. The contours get sharper. With sincere gratitude and prayers, she thanks the tree and the universe.

The water spirits whisper her name: "Milina, Milina", and together with the ripple from the brook a pleasant symphony is created. The now is love! A formation bestowed on the universe. It is quiet but still full of life. She lets out singing tones through her throat, but it really is the heart that opens up and the notes vibrate from her and are affected by everything and everyone. The wing movement from a little green bird is crystallized. She can feel it in her body. Nothing is separated from anything. No separation, only a great existing. One great consciousness. A responsibility to respond in the state of mind. Butterflies emerge and strengthen her figure and their nectar fills her with more nourishment. She needs the strength for her journey. Her goal becomes clear and, as if it has been decided long ago, now is her time. Nobody knows what lies ahead of her, not even she. Since fear cannot possibly exist in a state of love, she unsuspectingly follows the path. The connection to nature in the land without borders.

    Together.
    Affinity.
    Universe.

    A higher consciousness begins its journey down to earth.

Ann

She looked from the pile of newspapers on the floor to the bed. Bed. Newspapers. Her eyes moved as if she was watching a game of tennis. The papers called for her. Pick me! Read me! Ann would happily take one, cuddle up in bed and tightly embrace the newly mangled sheets. Read a few pages and see what was going on outside the hotel room. War, starving people, anything. People who lived, felt and experienced things. Somewhere.

Her inner paralysing weariness was depressing. She lived in a vacuum. Last night's dream was still lingering with both its smell and its sound. Ann could hear the train. She had to confess that the daydreams were brighter than life itself. The work as a chambermaid was hard. She stared at the pile of newspapers once again. The bed was made but she was late. Eric had personally asked her to take care of the Golden Suite. From now on, the suites were her responsibility.

"You can go home when you're done."

She was about to open her mouth to say that she wanted to work her six hours, but he cut in.

"You can still report a full day!"

The pitiful look had flashed in his eyes and the toad looking lips had formed a kiss. Why? Now was no time to think about that. During the few months she had worked here, she and the three Lithuanian girls had shared the responsibility for the rooms. It was an unwritten rule that they all left work at the same time. What was she supposed to say if Eric gave her a special treatment? She just had to take her time to get ready to leave.

It was an appealing thought, to pick up a newspaper. To do something different in her life, even though she had done just that when she applied for this job. Cleaning hotel rooms was something totally new. Ann could imagine how Samuel had pursed his lips when he heard that she would become a chambermaid instead of being a therapist. As if she had to account for what she did with her life to him. She sighed heavily and picked up the newspapers from the floor.

"Hello!"

"Sorry?" She turned towards the open door.

A handsome man, a few years older than her, was apparently waiting for an answer. He was staring at her, well shaved and with a pleasant look. What had he asked? She hadn't heard him.

"Excuse me? You were saying?"

"I asked if I can put my luggage in here before I check in? I heard that the cleaning wouldn't be finished until two o'clock today."

"Yes, of course. It will be done in about half an hour."
She reached out to take the bags, but the man persisted in
putting them in the closet himself.

"No, no." He got the suitcase in, smiled at her and held
his hand out to present himself.

"I don't think we've met before. John Leary, CEO." His
warm hand affected her. She felt a magnetic pull when his
eyes fixated her.

"I'm Ann. I started here in April."

"Are you working at the office?"

"I clean." She looked intently at him while his expression changed.

"Clean?" He inspected her from head to toe.

Ann had the same uniform as all the other maids. A
dull grey apron and a white shirt.

"Let me know when the room is ready. I'll be waiting
in the bistro."

The man gave her a short smile before he disappeared.
She nodded silently. A gentleman who had shown some interest at a first glance, but her title had disturbed his judge-
mental world. Why should she inform him personally? She
would send someone from the reception.

*"To fall in love after a separation: wait at least a year before you
get involved in a new relationship."*

How many times had she said that to her clients? It was so typical for her to feel attracted as soon as a man showed her the slightest interest. He had only been polite and nice, that didn't mean that he was interested in something more. She was starving to be seen.

Ann shook her head. The stress and lack of sleep made her absent-minded and distrait. For how long had she been standing in this room, starring at the pile of newspapers and the bed? She continued cleaning. Methodically. Structure and routines made her relax. Yet, she looked at her watch over and over again. Why the hurry? No one was waiting at home. That was painful.

A tear was burning behind her eye and she felt a need to talk to Charlotte as soon as she came home. Her allied. The friend who was always there, always supporting her. Charlotte could see straight through her and nailed the problem. Charlotte's easiness could also make Ann feel a bit envious. Did she really have the strength for that today? She scrolled through the list of contacts in her phone. Maybe she could call someone else? Which ones were still her friends? How many calls had she actually declined the last months? So easy, just a light touch on the display.

"Hey, girl. Happy and cheery I hear!"

"I'm sorry, but you know how it is. My whole body is aching and that doesn't go well with cleaning."

"I know, that's why I'm here. What do you want to do?"

"I just want to get into this newly made bed and never get up again", Ann laughed dryly.

"Yeah, I hear you. Don't you think we should do something fun? Go out? Saturdays are best, and you haven't been out for ages. You would feel awesome around normal people."

"I really don't know if I have the strength. I need to take a shower and then lie down with my legs elevated. My God, I'm almost fifty and totally busted. And I have to eat, I didn't have time for lunch."

"You eat, or you die. As well as having fun, that's a part of life, my friend."

"Oh, Eric asked me to take over the responsibility for the suites from now on, but I still get payed for my full six hours."

"So, he thinks he owns you now."

"Owns me?"

"Yes, he probably expects you to give something back in return."

"Ha! He can dream on! His best before-date expired a long time ago."

"Bloody men. Talk to you soon, but think about what I said about going out. Have a glass of wine and dance!"

Charlotte's happy voice lingered long after the conversation. Ann looked at the telephone, it seemed quieter than usual. Her clients had given up on her since she never returned their calls. In her mind, she could see their bewildered faces.

"Specialist in problematic relations?"

Her hand was trembling as she scrolled to Samuels number. The thirst was unbearable nowadays. Her lips were always dry and lip salves were strategically placed all around the apartment.

"We need to talk!" Her voice was more demanding than she had intended, and her hand was still trembling.

"Ann, I'm really tired. You must understand that! Why don't you call me after lunch tomorrow? I have a meeting that ends at one, okay?"

Samuel had already hung up before she got a chance to answer. Why did he keep on delaying their meeting? She was getting annoyed. There was a kind of dominance in his evasive way. *"You must understand that."* How many times had he not been tired? She remembered all the times he had given her a kiss on her forehead, before he firmly pushed her aside. All those times when she had been left there, standing with her arms hanging at her sides while he disappeared into the bedroom. She wanted to talk – he was too tired. The memories made her shiver. Now she started to understand: it was a pattern that could only lead to their separation.

The steam from the shower covered Ann when she opened the doors to the shower cabin and stepped over the pile of clothes on the floor. Thoroughly and scrupulously she let the dental floss work its way down between her teeth, just as the dental hygienist had so nicely instructed her. One tooth after the other. It felt good to focus on the flossing, even though her daily routines also gave her time to think.

The day had been awful, not at all what she had hoped for. The most tiring thing was all the sleepless nights, which had to come to an end. Ann hadn't woken up thoroughly rested in a long time. Sleeping pills – the thought was there. A false sleep. She also knew all too well what a lack of sleep could do to your body. Ann opened the wastepaper basket with the pedal and tossed down the string of dental floss. She wanted to get a good night's sleep tonight, she was exhausted. She lay down on the sofa and pulled the cover over her body. Wrapped herself up in it as if she needed extra protection. She was met by the smell of somebody else's detergent. Ann didn't like the launderette, maybe she should by a washing machine? Her finances would be stable when the house and the summer house had been valued. They also had the boat and two cars, all of which was part of their joint property. Of that, half was hers. The apartment she sublet had a reasonable rent in spite of the location. She had been lucky.

All thoughts put her in a trance and she could no longer decide where to begin or what she wanted. An enormous weariness fell over her. It was as if she couldn't figure out her next move. The thoughts rushed through her head as if there wasn't a reasonable clue to be found. She was unable to make a clear decision and the sleep eluded her. In the small hours she went in to the bedroom, fell down on her bed and into a dreamless slumber.

The alarm on the phone woke her up. It took a while before she turned it off. She must have been sleeping, despite everything, she thought and pressed snooze. The morning light felt dark and gloomy outside. Now she woke up divorced, alone, and the confusion crept up on her. It was ironic that she now went through all the faces of a separation that she'd only been talking about. She must have guided hundreds of couples through their divorces by now. Even if they had not all been dramatic, the phases were there. This lack of stability was all new to her. The curiosity on life, the people and the meetings in between. Everything that she had loved was lost. She had made the decision to stop working as a therapist to try to find her way back to life. But when she managed to fall asleep, she always woke up with a dry mouth and a feeling of being locked up in a hopeless state.

The morning traffic had begun out on the streets. Life painfully continued outside the window. She couldn't get used to the dull thoughts that weighed her down. The silence in the apartment was so close and got a grip on her. She stretched her body. The double bed felt unnecessarily big. She missed the small feet that had tiptoed into the room during the child years. Morning cuddles with the whole family in bed. They had called Cayla 'miss all over the place'. The little one had taken most space with her resolute, striking and dominating ways. Ann couldn't deny the big loss that ached in her heart. The family. Her little tribe here on earth. Her child, Cayla. So proud and straight forward. Simon, her little treasure. Warm, safe and cuddly. What would the future be like?

She was going to meet Cayla after work today. Cayla, who stood on her own two feet now. She was turning eighteen in a couple of months. Mother and daughter. Rat and cat.

She dressed slowly. The trousers were a mess, and she changed to a skirt. Switched to jeans. Tried on three tops before it felt okay. It still didn't feel good! She stared at her clothes with disappointment. She didn't have any style anymore. It was in exactly these situations that the confusion hit her. She can't reach a decision on either this or that. She puts some mascara on her eyelashes. She wants to look lively for Cayla. She used to be Mrs Bennett with her own clinic at East Park. She was sought for, always fully booked. A specialist in family issues and relationships. Her reputation was good. What did they say about her now? Could others see the temporary paralysis she seemed to experience every time she tried to decide something? Her inability to know. The feeling of not knowing made her worried. The confident and calm woman seemed to have checked out.

Today she cleans the rooms harder, as if it would go quicker or be cleaner at the hotel. It's nice to be alone, but yet have people around. To be part of a greater whole. Her thoughts go around and round. She thinks a lot about Cayla. How is she? What does she feel? She's never had the same telepathic contact with her daughter as she has with Cayla's older brother, Simon. There had already been a distance to Cayla during the pregnancy. With a horrified feeling, she had felt like she only lent her body to someone already stronger than herself. As if the baby was offended by her. Samuel got more and more absent the more her stomach grew, as if the bump distanced even him. She had diminished him the bigger the stomach got. Samuel had made her pregnant with Cayla while she was asleep. It bothered her deep inside. The only one she had admitted it to, was Charlotte.

Charlotte had raised an eyebrow, put her lips together and stared at her.

"You were asleep?"

"Yes. I was lying face down and woke up from a burning sensation. When he pulled it out."

"And?"

"He said he was sorry and fell asleep right away."

"What did he say he was sorry for?"

"He knows that I don't want to have sex in that way."

"Has it happened before?"

"It may have."

"May have? Ann, this is serious! Was it the first time?"

"It has happened before. We've talked about it, that I don't want to."

"But he still does it? Stop biting your cheek, Ann!"

"He says it's because I drive him crazy."

"And you believe him?"

"Apparently."

"I think that you're just too much of a coward to stand up for yourself! That's what I think. Rape, that's what it is. Do you hear me? Rape!"

"It was rape!" She had looked determined. Her eyes had flashed.

Ann felt nervous and looked at her watch several times while she sat at the café and waited. Could she have gotten the day or time wrong? She didn't want to call and flipped randomly through a newspaper. When she looked up again, Cayla was standing in the doorway. She leaned her head towards the doorframe. Her outgrown pink fringed coat only covered half way down her thighs. She was wearing a pair of tights in different light blue colours and it looked as if her legs were two meters long. She was so beautiful. Cayla had always had a certain glow around her.

So whole.

So clean.

Angel like.

Cayla spotted Ann and walked towards her in smooth moves. Her long limbs swung a little. Toes first, then the whole foot. A catwalk. Their daughter had got the best of them both.

"Hi, sweetheart." Ann tried to smile bright.

"Hi, Mum."

A quick and casual hug. They both take a seat. Ann fights her indefinable tears.

Betrayal – longing – forgetfulness – lack of sleep.

"Shall we have a cup of coffee?"

"Mum, do you really think I want to drink coffee this late? I thought we could eat!"

Cayla locks her gaze on her, just as Ann has seen her do so many times. She nervously chewes on the inside of her cheek. A bad habit that has resulted in a little lump.

"You look tired, Mum."

"I do?" She smiles, a bit surprised of her answer. She knows that she looks tired. The grey is taking over.

"Dad is never at home. I have to cook my own food all the time."

Cayla pouts with her lips and looks discouraged down on a couple of grains of maize.

"Isn't he at home? So, is he working late, or what?"

Couldn't he wait before he met someone new?

"I don't know what he's doing. He never has time to eat or talk. Why can't you stay in the house and he move out?"

"Do you want that?"

"I want everything to be as it was before, don't you get that? I want a normal family. I don't want to be the child of divorced parents, someone who nobody cares about."

"Do I understand this right, you feel like no one cares about you?"

"Oh, Mum, why do you have to talk like a therapist? Can't you just be normal!"

My body is tired when I walk home. The apartment feels small and impersonal. I fix the laundry. The floor is filled with all the clothes I have tried on. The clothes that don't fit my body. I fetch a bin bag and decide to give three pairs of trousers and two blouses to the charity shop. I feel sick when I see the sofa. I take a long shower. Stare into the fridge. The dry millet salad I ate wasn't enough, even though it had cost a fortune. The dressing is going up and down and gives me heartburn. What did I usually do when I came home? I tirelessly made sure that our home was perfect. I liked my life. So, I thought. I called a friend, re-scheduled an appointment. Ironed a shirt. I did all that without getting tired. I was so capable! The table was set at five thirty. The whole pack gathered.

I feel successful. I've made a fresh salad from organic produce. I've tried a new recipe I've seen in a magazine: a rich Louisiana casserole with peppers, sweetcorn, spicy sausages and crayfish. I sprinkle the food with a whole pot of parsley. It has beautiful colours.

"It tastes good", he says. I glance at him and continue to chew. A little thoughtful after the whole day. He must have a lot on his mind. Documents, e-mails, meetings and trips. He doesn't tell me a lot these days. However, I think I know everything. Endless days at the office. He does all that to keep the family together. Five days a week. Sometimes extra hours in the weekends.

"Do you have to put parsley on it? You know I don't like that!"

Cayla's voice is a bit too treble. It's a statement, and I know I've made a mistake. I bite my cheek. Simon sees it.

"I think it is delicious, Mum. I will probably starve to death when I move out."

His smile is big. My wonderful boy. One day he will no longer be here. It will be very empty.

"You've been too spoiled", Samuel says. Suddenly with total presence. He looks at them both. "How will you manage on your own?"

He smiles at me. His eyes sparkle. I love it when he does that, when he joins in with all his power. Says things. Takes care of life. It makes me feel successful and feminine.

"I've been thinking about buying a cheap apartment,

then I will renovate it and sell it at a profit. Use the money to buy a new one, renovate again, and keep on doing it until I can afford a house." Simon talks with food in his mouth.

"So, you think that you will be able to get a bank loan and buy an apartment just because you're studying construction, do you?" Cayla picks demonstratively her sausage pieces and the parsley to the side.

I'm happy that she eats a little. Every bite feels like a relief.

"Then I'll get a proper job. The building sights have high demands for people like me." He flexes with his arm muscles.

"You are such a drip!" Cayla puts down her knife and fork with a bang. "You're all so embarrassing!"

Samuel touches my foot with his. We cannot hold back our smiles. I hold my napkin to my mouth.

"Does anyone want some ice cream? Did you think the casserole was to spicy?"

Who am I without my family?

Ann

Her feet are stuck. The sharp heels sneer at her. The room is spinning. There insn't enough air. It smells of smoke. She has to get out. If she only could see which door she came in through. How will she get out? There is no air in here. She crawls. The wall. If she finds a wall, she can find the door. Doors are in walls. Someone is staring at her. Thera are several people in the room. How did they get in? Where is the door out? Don't touch me! Her body aches. Leve me alone! Now they're talking. What are they saying? Someone stops her. Several hands pull her back into the smoke. Someone is holding a hand over her mouth. The air runs out. She tries to scream. She screams and falls. She hurts herself. Crawls. Here comes the train. The sound drowns her call for help. The train splits her. Two halves. She doesn't feel anything. If only the smoke could dissipate so she can find her high heels.

Ann wakes up. The heart is pounding as if she's been running for miles, hunted by a tiger. She hurries out of bed. Her mouth is dry and the glass on the coffee table is already empty. She can't remember that she's been drinking during the night. The dreams are there to stay. The stiffness aches in her body. She drinks two glasses of ice-cold water by the sink. She lets her hands glide along her body to make sure that it's intact. The skin is sticky from night perspiration. She slowly rocks her body back and forth to try to find a soothing pace. What are the dreams trying to tell her? Do they have a message? She needs to talk to someone, make an appointment. Get professional help.

The air that hits her is colder than she has expected when the door shuts behind her. It felt nice to get away from home and to get her body moving. She has to admit it's nice that it's Monday again. The weekends have become a part of her pain. They feel endless now when she has so much time. Time makes her realize the failure, how wrong it has all become. She needs to think some thoughts to their ends. Look back at her life. Why? How? About? All of that which Charlotte said she should skip. Charlotte would already have gotten herself a 'catch and release', and uninhibited enjoyed a man's body. From one to the next. That was her right as a free woman. Yes, she could be a bit envious over all that lightness Charlotte had. That playful easiness.

Ann didn't have a wish to meet someone new. The pure thought of it was absurd. The inspiration and the feeling of breathing in life, was what she wanted to find her way back to. She had lost herself somewhere along the road. Sold herself out. It wasn't a longing for the old, rather something vague in front of her that she sought. It was there, far away, even though diffuse. There was so much that she had let slip away, so much she didn't care for anymore. Things. It

42

didn't matter if she washed her hair in a cheap shampoo or that her pair of scissors didn't have a specific place in the kitchen drawer. Come to think of it, all of that had been Samuel's suggestions.

All the how-when-where-settling, and she had just followed like a loyal dog. So much like a typical woman. Compromising. *Oh, you want to go there on holiday? Okay, pizza tonight!* She'd done it and done it: stopped asking herself if it was right or felt right by her. Small steps that took her further away from the person she was meant to be. So much that she had lost herself in a relationship that ended with a few words.

"I want a divorce!"

The words had cut through her, made her lose her foothold. The thought made her shiver. The lump that had grown when he formed the words with his lips, yet it was no surprise. How many times hadn't she had that thought herself? All of a sudden it was all in flames and the fire couldn't be put out. It was too late. Something had been burning long before that, but now nothing could be saved ...

The children.

The house.

The garden.

Everything that had meant so much to her, that which they'd had together, was annihilated. All plans for the future were ruined.

"I want a divorce!" Then he had brought up everything

she lacked as a woman.

She went around the hotel corner. The service entrance was on the side of the building. She said hello to two Lithuanian women.

"Sure, the weekend has been nice."

If I only could be spared my nightmares.

"Eric wants to talk to you. He said that you can go up to his office."

Was it just imagination, or did they exchange glances behind her back? She changed her clothes and locked her belongings into the locker. She took the stairs to the office.

Eric's desk was cluttered with papers. He looked up and asked her to sit down. There was a jacket on the chair and she hung it over the armrest. Oddly enough, she felt nervous and didn't know where to look. Had she not been doing a good job? She tried to act logically. He seemed a bit stressed. She needed this job to be able to pay her rent and sort out her life. She meets Eric's gaze. He was known to be tough and hard, but also fair. Rumours said that he was extremely strong and had a sense of humour.

"How do you like it here?"

"Very well!"

"You used to work as a psychologist?"

"Therapist, I'm trained in conversational therapy."

Specialized in couples' therapy, ironically.

"Why aren't you doing that for a living?"

"I applied for this job and like it here."

It was obvious that her answer wouldn't be enough. Eric raised his eyebrows.

"So what, you didn't make it financially?"

It had nothing to do with my finances.

What did he want? He apparently had a problem with her working as a chambermaid.

"I don't understand, why did you quit?"

Eric had raised his tone a little. She noticed that but tried not to catalogue and diagnose him. She easily fell into the therapist role, a biproduct. She was also a good listener and knew what to say to wake up the right line of thoughts and to get the person to feel taken care of during their meeting. It was easy for her to steer the conversation.

"Why did you quit your other job? Didn't you do well?" Eric looked smug and leaned back in his chair.

She started to feel annoyed. It was something with his look that made her feel uneasy. What was he trying to say? Why couldn't he speak up? She was here to sort out and put her past in order, her inner self.

"I like it here."

That was at least partially true.

"What? Are you divorced?"

"Yes, that's right, and I wanted to try something else."

"Isn't it better if you get yourself a new husband who can provide for you?" Eric blew out his chest.

She looked surprised at him. The tongue was burning, eager to deliver a snide comment. She bit the lump in her cheek. What did she have to gain from a comment like that? To pay back. What would that lead to? Was it worth it?

"Men are like little boys, never forget that." Her mother's voice echoed.

All of a sudden everything went still in her and she became aware of a new, tingling sensation. Instead of being upset, feelings bubbling like sparkling wine filled her. A vent that was on its way to open up – a sensation of bubbling laughter. She smiled. The laughter was near. Eric looked at her, worried, and tilted his chair nervously.

"Yes, maybe. Was there something else? I would like to get to work."

Eric lost the thread, mumbled something about them being pleased with her and went back to moving the papers around on the desk.

A bubbling laughter worked its way up and she was quick to close the door behind her. Her eyes giggled at her in the mirror in the elevator. When she was new on the job her body had ached. All the old had left her body. Feelings of unreality, fragments from the past with Samuel. Small pieces of memories from her life that she didn't quite understand how they had been created. The eyes, unable to meet hers when he came home. Yet, she had thought that they'd had a good life. Arranged that little extra to their cosy dinners. Flowers in the kitchen. She arranged for the children to be at home. Sometimes they made love in the way that she thought it had to be after two childbirths and a long relationship. He turned his back to her afterwards, but she cuddled up behind and caressed him until she heard the familiar breaths. She loved his smell. The sounds from his body. After all the years. She didn't understand anything else back then. Not until the words became reality. Get a divorce. Division of the joint property of husband and wife. Dissolution of marriage. Been living on him. When she thought about it, it felt like a film about somebody else's life. Another woman's drama on tv. Had Eric hinted that she wouldn't be able to support herself as a single? Samuel had also said that she'd been living on him, that was what he had said. Feeding off of him, like a parasite. An amoeba that had slowly choked him.

It was unusually calm today. The traffic was still quiet. She glanced at her watch. She was early. A couple of sparrows had found some crumbs at East Park. A great tit accompanied them. A bag of empty cans was hidden under the bench. She studied the sparrows. They made her think of how she had lived. Though she had rather wandered about like an upset hen. She had thought that was how one took on life. By giving she would receive. If she received, she would be fulfilled herself. So, she had continued living, elaborate, a bit careful but still wandering about. Had she been happy? No, if anything it had been a long, drawn out compromise to make everything work, to keep it together. She was that great tit trying to be a sparrow. The illusion she had built was to just try to live, to desperately stay in the struggle.

A moped turned in on the gravel. The flock of sparrows flew up in a tree. She went on along the road towards Greenville Market. A bit further ahead she saw a lonely mother with a pram and a dog. The mother looked stressed, pulled the leash and tried to walk in the other direction with the pram. There was no sound coming from it, maybe she wanted to come home and get some sleep herself. Maybe someone was waiting for her back home. The stress. The compromising. She felt it. She had lived it her whole adult life.

The permissive silence – but what about me?

She had clenched her teeth until they started to ache. She had bitterly shaved her legs for the Saturday evening. Cooked something extra nice. Studied the wines in the magazines. Had bought organic meat at the Farmers Market. All to satisfy something outside herself. To get something in return. To get laid to feel good enough to be a wife. If she didn't do all that, the shame woke up. She could hear Samuel's wordless communication when the laundry basket spilled over. When the washing-up was still in the dishwasher. So, she went on. The doing became a way of life. In the end, she hadn't noticed it, but she had slowly turned into a martyr, and she made sure it got its space. Samuel had his own expression when he wasn't happy with what she had done. It could be things that weren't placed where they should be or if there were still stains on the clothes. Small, petty details that could turn into quarrels that prolonged a whole week. The power struggles.

She rounded the corner to Harbour Road. Inhaled the smell of the sea breeze. She looked jealously at the houseboats. It would be so easy in a little boat. To live on just a few square meters. A couple of months ago she'd had a

house that was three hundred square meters with a garden
and a garage for two cars. And a summer house. One or
two trips abroad per year. Her own car.

Charlotte hugged Ann and held the door to the café.
The smell of coffee and buns met them.

Homely.

Warm.

Sheltered.

They talked and sat down at a table. The café was empty, except for a man who was deeply absorbed in a book.
He raised his eyes and let his gaze glide over Charlotte's
tight jeans.

"Do you want coffee?"

"A cappuccino with soy milk."

Ann looked at Charlotte. Always so perfect. Her
straight white teeth. Pretty little freckles on her nose. Thick
blond braids. She looked both young and mature. She wore
a thin light blue sweater. She could see a white lace bra and
the contours of her breasts. Ann never dressed that provocative. Charlotte licked the cream off her bun.

"Are you sure you don't want to try some? You can
have a bite." She slid the plate over with a giving gesture.

Ann slowly shook her head. She didn't want any.
The cream would make her stomach turn inside out. She
changed focus.

"Tell me now! You were out last night but look so fresh.
How do you do it?"

"Thanks. You are so sweet!"

50

Charlotte fidgeted on her braids. Licked the cream off her lips.

"It was great. He was there again. You know, the man I met last time." She leaned forward and lowered her voice. "I think he's married, but we talked a little anyway. He got my number. He'll probably call soon."

"What makes you think he's married?"

"By the way he looked at me and waited, not just helped himself. I think it's sexy when men do that. Don't you?"

They both laughed.

"No, I haven't really thought about it."

"Maybe it's about time you did? So, are you coming out with me tonight?"

Her whole body screamed no, but so much had happened since she started saying yes. Charlotte had encouraged her. Say yes instead of no. She practiced it in the grocery shop. No to apples but yes to avocado. What else could her body say yes to?

"I'll think about it!"

Ann was fascinated by the fact that Charlotte always managed to catch the guys. It made no difference if they were married. To Ann, life should be correct. A married man is a married man, which was the same as dangerous grounds.

"You really should come with me soon. You need to do something fun. A little sex would cheer you up."

Ann coughed and almost swallowed her coffee the wrong way.

"Oh, my God, you act as if you're an old spinster. You're not a virgin, are you?" More laughter.

"But you really need to put life into your feminine side. Bring out the real woman in you."

"It sounds so easy when you say it. I just feel so tired. Sex doesn't feel interesting."

"You need to step out of that role of martyrdom and put that relationship behind you. Believe me! You'll wear yourself out. It's as if you think that the two of you will get back together again. It won't be that way! You have to realize that soon! Close that door, love."

Ann stared into her cup. The foam had mixed with the coffee.

"No, I know that there's no us anymore. But I hope that we will find a way to communicate with each other."

"Have you ever been able to do that? Honestly! Tell me the truth, have you ever been able to communicate?"

"No."

"Let go of him. Make an active choice. Start filling your life with what's good instead. Say yes to your femininity. Start asking yourself: Who am I as a free person? Who am I as a woman? What do I enjoy? Who am I sexually? What do I like? Let go of all previous conceptions!"

"I don't think I'm ready for that yet."

"Come on! You are as ready as ever. Do it now before you hit your best before-date. This is the right time for you to start exploring your own body!"

Charlotte leaned closer to Ann. She could feel the warmth from her friend's body when she leaned in. A vague scent of something she couldn't name. A sunny day or a lawn with playing children. To Charlotte everything was easy. But also, attractive. She had always thought that Charlotte had that thing she wouldn't dare herself: that flirtatious and open-minded way. Men saw her. Always. Everywhere. They had been interrailing together before Ann met Samuel and she'd had a busy time keeping her eye on Charlotte. Eye contact. Flirts and close contacts. Waiters. Business men. Those glittering blue eyes could trap any man.

It was as if Charlotte heard her thoughts.

"Once you start appreciating your beautiful body, others will to. The body harbours you heart! When you take care of your body your heart will listen extra carefully. At least think about it. Start saying yes to the woman in you!"

She leaned even a little closer over the table and lowered her voice a little extra.

"Start by caressing your nipples every night. Caress them! You'll see what happens. Awesome!" She leaned back and took a big bite of her cream bun. That was yet another thing that she really envied her friend. Charlotte could eat anything and yet have a perfect body.

"Don't look so shocked. You'll love me even more after this. I'll get you going!"

They laughed. Which was perfect, since Ann didn't have to reveal her embarrassment. She was just about to ask for more coffee when the telephone rung. It said 'Cayla' on the display. She felt a tug in her heart. Was it something she had promised her? Her guilty feelings woke up by just seeing the name.

"Hi, sweetheart!"

"Mum, where are you?"

Her voice was strained, a tone of guilt. It would soon come, the tirade about how she was not good enough. What had she forgotten? She searched desperately in her memory.

"You were supposed to come to the stables today and see me compete. Where are you? I could actually need some help!"

"I'm on my way, honey. I'm coming! As I said, I'm on my way. I just got held up. Is your dad there? I'm coming."

"Yes, he drove me. He's got a car!"

There it was: he has a car. He doesn't forget. Yes, he kept the car, the house and the children. She wanted to say that, but she kept quiet.

"I'll soon be there, darling."

She hung up. All the laughter was gone. "I have to take a taxi to the stables. Apparently, there's a competition. How could I forget that?"

"Okay, good luck. Don't lose yourself, and don't forget that about your breasts."

A quick goodbye.

She barely made it in time.

54

The silence was like a wall when she opened her apartment door. Ann hesitated a second before she stepped over the threshold. Was this her home? A short stop while she waited for the next move. She sank down to the floor. Shoulders and hips were aching from physical work. She'd been working hard all week long and should welcome the weekend. She leaned her head against the wall and took a few deep breaths.

When the thought doesn't demand to be thought, silence appears.

She dropped all her clothes on the floor. A luxurious freedom she thought had disappeared during her teenage years. Now, the piles of clothes seamed to pop up like mushrooms after the rain. She took a long shower, let the water wash away the day. The hot steam in the bathroom created a mist on the mirror. She wiped it away with the palm of her hand. Charlotte's words had woken up something inside of her. To say yes to life. And now caress her breasts. She touched them carefully. Her breasts. Now they were only hers. Two breasts. Two children. She had breastfed them for a long time. At that time, she had learnt to appreciate her breasts as something practical. She wiped away more of the mist so both her breasts became visible in the mirror. At her age, one was supposed to study one's breasts and do a mammography. Search for lumps. Practical do-it-yourself-notes at the obstetrician's clinic. Her breasts looked familiar, yet not. She slowly touched them with both hands. Caressed them. The nipples quickly stiffened. It had been a long time since Samuel had cupped his big hands over them and fondly tightened his grip. A shiver went through her body. She had liked the way he'd touched her breasts. It had made her feel feminine, as if she had something he didn't have. Ann had never been able to enjoy her body in full, always focused on the flaws. Samuel was the only one she had let in a bit further. A long relationship, and then, the betrayal. She didn't have the strength to be reminded again. She must stop thinking of him, just like Charlotte had said. Stop thinking of the image of him by the stable and his expression when she had said no to a lift home, that she wanted to walk. Cayla's short hug and pitiful look when the car drove away. Newly washed and polished. It was over! He would never more touch her body. Was the telephone ringing? She quickly let go of her breasts.

”Hello?”

”Hi, Mum!”

”Simon?”

”What are you doing? You sound so surprised?”

”I do? I just got out of the shower.”

"You sound so strange. Kevin and I are at the front door. We're coming up for a while."

Typical Simon. And who was Kevin?

"Yes, sure. I have to put some clothes on."

"But you sound so strange. Are you alone?"

"Yes, of course! Come on in."

Company? She felt ill at ease and tired. Simon was one thing, but someone she didn't know? She had never heard of Kevin. In just a few months she had lost contact with her children. For twenty-one years she had known Simon's friends. She put on a pair of sweatpants and a hoodie. Closed the door to the bedroom.

"Hi, Mum!"

Simon gave her a warm hug. Held her for a while, like he always did. She breathed in his familiar scent, so subtle and mild, hidden beneath the other smells. His stubble felt rough against her cheek. He had become a grown man, but to her he would always be her little boy.

"Mum, this is Kevin. My friend. I wanted you to meet him."

She held out her hand. The young man took a step into the hall. Gave her a hug. Another kind of embrace, softer, but yet that little squeezing feeling. Another scent. Sweeter. Vanilla.

"Do come in."

"We were going to an Indian restaurant in the neighbourhood and then to a bar."

"I'm glad you came by."

She met Kevin's eyes again. He held hers. An intense intimate gaze. Her cheeks got warm.

"Come in!"

Now that they were here, she'd better make the best of it. Simon reached for the remote and switched off the tv. She would ask him to show how it worked. She turned off the tv and put it on by unplugging and re-inserting the plug.

"How are you, Mum? You look a little tired."

"I'm fine. Don't worry."

She tried to smile and ran her hand through her wet hair. Did she look tired? She'd worked hard. Once she fell asleep it took several hours to wake up. Her walks to work forced the body to start up again.

"Cayla competed this weekend." It was easier to talk about something else.

"I spoke to her." He rolled his eyes and made a neighing sound.

A warmth spread in her chest. It always felt easier with Simon around.

"Cool apartment!" Kevin looked around with confidence. Those eyes again. Intensive green. Long thick eyelashes.

"I sublet. Furnished", she added almost apologetically. "It's not really my taste. Too old fashioned and the furniture and the curtains are too dark." She stroked the brown leather sofa with one hand. "I prefer lighter colours, pastels.

If the apartment was mine, I would change everything to lighter wood ...”

The words lingered. She stopped in the middle of the sentence. She had just parked here. Couldn't bother to think about how it would be later on.

”I like it, it's homely”, Kevin said.

It looked as if he liked it. He seemed to be an honest person who said what he thought.

”Simon has told me that you're newly separated”, he said unconstrainedly and sat down in the sofa. Simon dropped down next to him. She still thought of him as a little boy. He'd gotten an apartment from his father when they separated. From daddy, not her.

She secretly studied Kevin. Long slim fingers. Maybe he was wearing make-up, it was hard to tell in the dark. Maybe he had natural dark lines around his eyes, maybe he came from a Mediterranian family? He was very beautiful. His features reminded her of a woman she'd known but who's name she'd forgotten. He had put one leg over the other. Simon sat leaning forward with his elbows on his legs. Didn't let his eyes off her.

”Can I get you something?”

”Do you have beer?”

”No”, she laughed. ”But I actually think I have wine. Red or white?”

They both wanted red. It felt good to go out to the small kitchen. She had never cooked any food there. She was afraid of the gas cooker. Afraid that it would leak. It took a while to find the corkscrew. Three glasses. She was going to take a sip of wine. Try to relax. Be the relaxed newly separated mum who offered her son and his friend some wine. It was so nice that they came by.

Simon and Kevin sat close to each other in the sofa and watched something in a mobile phone. Their heads touched.

"We're ordering pizza. Do you want one?"

"I thought you were going to have Indian? No, thank you. Order a Greek salad for me."

It was close to midnight when they left. She said no several times to join them but appreciated that they'd asked. She liked the way Kevin's steady gaze held her. His firm hug at the door. The wine had made her relax. Relaxed with control. She poured herself the last of the wine and sat down in the sofa. She needed to get the night sorted out. She had laughed in a way she hadn't done in a long while. She couldn't be falling in love with her son's friend! She realized that she was a bit tipsy. She felt uncomfortably dizzy, but the intoxication had a softening effect. All of that which felt harsh and artificial in her life felt distant. Every sip of wine made her life easier, like when old plaque was dissolved, and the inside of the mouth got cleaner. It had been liberating with a bottle of wine and good company. She had always been drinking with great respect. She knew it could be a hard-earned experience to seek help in the bottle, but this feeling made her want more. A state of being. To surrender to the intoxication of alcohol. To give in. Was this a way for her to move on? Let the wine soften everything and clean out all the old. Dare to make room for her dreams again?

She opened another bottle. Put on some music and danced.

Free.

Naked.

Joy.

The drunkenness came over her when she was in bed. The hope that had been there during the evening changed into anxiety. The feeling of saying yes was gone. She knew all too well how life could be destroyed by alcohol. But the intoxication was stronger than her thoughts. The harsh and worn surface was on its way back. Mental pictures of Kevin turned up and she realized how she had tried all evening to push them away. It was probably imagination. His hungry eyes that had framed her. The dark thick eyelashes that had found their way into her fervour. His small-boned hands that she'd had trouble not to look at. She imagined how Kevin's hand slowly explored under her nightgown, caressing her breasts. Sensitive fingers. She imagined running her fingers through his hair. Men at her age had no hair. She fell asleep. Woke up at four, soaked in sweat.

She fell asleep again and woke up late in the morning. When was the last time she'd slept this long? Her mouth was dry. The thoughts went back to the night with Simon and Kevin. Thinking about Kevin made her lighter, she had to admit that, though she was going to keep that to herself. What was she doing, thinking about a man so much younger than herself? She hovered between just keeping him in her thoughts, to being locked in an embrace. Those thoughts made her feel worthy. As if she was good enough.

Charlotte

"Are you sure you don't want to come?"

"Absolutely", a sleepy Ann answered.

Charlotte rolled her eyes and made a face when she put down the phone. Ann was so boring when she never wanted to do anything, and she could be such a know-all sometimes. Humdrum and boring. As if Ann's life would be better by lying in a rented sofa, unable to sleep! She was still living in the past. She let the subconscious control her.

"So what!" Charlotte didn't have any problems going out on her own. On the contrary, she liked it. She knew what to do to avoid feeling alone and new all the opening lines by now. After a couple of glasses of wine, the repertoire came by itself. She needed some extra excitement tonight. She put on the little black dress. A favourite that always worked. She raised the volume while she put on her make-up. The wineglass stood on the edge of the bathtub and she drank the last of it before she brushed her teeth. Ann didn't know what she was missing.

It was noisy and crowded. The music was so loud that she hardly heard her own thoughts when she jostled her way to the bar. Payday weekend, maybe she should

have chosen another bar tonight? It didn't take long for her
to notice him. He looked so neat and fresh. A couple of
years younger than her. Maybe out with colleagues from
work. A well-behaved gang out to get a couple of beers too
many, maybe a whiskey or two would follow. They were not
the kind of people who would get drunk and insufferable.
That was what she was looking for.

Their eyes met when he leaned forward to yell something into a friend's ear. He held her gaze. Good looking
hair that curled in the nape of his neck. Looking good. A
perfect catch in other words. She let go of his gaze with a
smile and tried to get the attention of a bartender.

Another man left room for her.

"Alone tonight?"

She didn't bother answering him but appreciated that
he let his eyes move over her body. She liked it when men
looked at her. It made her feel noticed, beautiful, as if she
had a right to her feminine side. It held power. She was
the one in control. Captain of the ship. Sometimes she had
thought about talking to Ann about it, but she couldn't
stand Ann's psychological models to explain it. Oh, she
needed more wine.

"A glass of rosé, please."

The bartender lingered with his gaze on her alluring
plunging neckline. Apparently, it worked. She saw that the
man she'd had a look at was already on his way towards
her. One glance and he was ready. Sometimes she wished it

was more of a challenge. She left her credit card in the bar but new that someone else would pay later. That was part of the plan. She wondered if the bartender had learnt her tricks by now. They must be experts on people as the wee hours sucked the honesty of alcohol out of people. Or was that only in the movies?

All of a sudden, she had a déjà vu. A flutter in her stomach and she reached for something. A memory? Did she mix all the nights out together? Was it the alcohol that reminded her of her rotten childhood? All of a sudden everything was spinning.

"Are you alright?" His voice was warm. He had caught her. He continued without waiting for an answer. "Come, you need some air."

She felt wobbly on her high heels, but he had a firm grip around her waist. Almost carrying her in his strong arms. She felt small and helpless but let herself get dragged out through the crowd.

Outside it was cool and Charlotte shivered. He took off his sweater. Pulled it over her head. It smelled expensive aftershave and a hint of fabric softener.

"What happened? You went pale. I thought you would faint!"

He smiled. He was good looking! His voice woke something in her. She felt a little embarrassed and looked down at his arm that was still lying safely around her waist. She had lost herself in there, lost control. The rudder had been torn from her and she had capsized. Why?

"Can I let go?"

She nodded vaguely. Her tongue didn't really want to form any words. She, who always gave everyone tit for tat. He affected her.

"It's nice to get out, you can't hear anything in there!" He pointed at a café across the street. "Shall we go over there and sit down for a while."

She nodded again and realized that she really wanted his arm back around her waist. She must look terrible in that big sweater. It was expensive. Maybe lambswool. There was an emblem, but she didn't dare to look down and see what it said, so she focused on walking straight.

He held up the door in a polite way. She dropped down in one of the armchairs directly inside the door. The place was empty except for a younger couple with a pram next to a table. She imagined they were on their way home after they had been to the paediatrics emergency ward. But what did she know? There was a story behind every face.

"Stay here, I'll be right back. The beer just runs right through me." He hurried towards the toilet. He must be almost two meters tall, she thought. His back was muscular. This was her chance to sneak away. Put his sweater on the chair and disappear. It felt like a bad drama. She also had to get back to get her credit card in the bar. Her thoughts were spinning. She needed to take control again. He wasn't the right type of man. He didn't just want to get laid. She felt misplaced in his sweater. She took up her mirror from her handbag. The make-up looked god. The hair was okay. Her eyes looked a bit nervous and she exhaled.

"You dropped something!" He was back and pointed at something on the floor.

She bent down to pick it up. The plastic covering around the condom seemed to glow against the floor. Had he seen what it was? She'd put several in her handbag. She had been horny tonight and thought that she should be able to get laid at least twice. Different men. Never twice with the same man. Now that felt like a distant bad tv-show.

"What would you like? I'm starving! We were on a business dinner and only had a small portion of fish. Tasted good, yes – satisfying, no."

She realized she still hadn't opened her mouth, but he seemed to understand her gesticulating arms and incoherent phrases about the credit card that was still in the bar.

"Of course I'll pay! What kind of man would drag a woman out on the street without buying?" He smiled that smile again, a small dimple showed on the right side. He looked even younger now, maybe he was just over thirty. Hard to tell. He had a boyish charm.

"They will soon be closing", he said and turned up with two cappuccinos and two prawn sandwiches.

"I also took these", he said and held out two pieces of cake. "Chocolate cake, I thought you might like that."

"Thanks, that's my favourite!"

"I guessed that."

The dimple was back! She smiled but shyly bit her lip when he focused on eating the prawn sandwich. She was in control again, even if she didn't know in what direction she was going.

Estrid

Estrid looked up at the sun that stood high in the sky, it wasn't a good time to arrive. She wished she had time to do her chores. Her sister would have to work hard without her. She put her hand to her stomach. The nutcracker whispered in her ear:

Today mother
your child will be born.

She squatted down and waited for the next contraction. The wave rolled in over her and reminded her body of what was coming. She rested her eyes on a mountain ash. The red berries were glowing against the cloudless sky. It was still too early, but it wouldn't take long before they could collect the rowanberries. The autumn was clear and it was a comfortable temperature during the nights. She inhaled the air. Stood up and walked back to the camp. If she was lucky the contractions would subside like they had with her third child and start in the evening again. Lingonberries, rosehips and acorns. Hazelnuts and mushrooms, it was a lot to collect. She was needed before the winter. May the birth be quick this time. When the men were gone the women needed to stay together. The loss of the child last month was still hanging over them. Sigrid's stillborn boy had also been malformed. Then the febrile convulsions had taken over the mother's body. Not a good sign. They had prayed and sacrificed the last pig to Eir and the healing herbs had finally saved Sigrid.

She tried to shake off the images of the deformed child when the next contraction came. She saw her sister in a distance. A couple of young boys were playing by the fire.

"Elida!"

Her sister immediately let go of the firewood she held in her arms and rushed to her. The memory of Sigrid's dead son was hanging like a fog over the women.

"It will still take a while! But ask the younger ones to start heating the water."

Estrid leaned into the big house. The smoke stung her eyes and the sharp smell made her stomach turn inside out. She threw up the gruel she'd had for breakfast. A couple of hens hurried up to eat it. She was going to give birth to her baby outside. She let the contraction fade away while she crouched down again, and then went around the house. The baby was pushing down. Bearing-down contractions already? It would go quickly this time. Maybe she could be up and about as soon as tonight and help them clean the mushrooms. She hoped nothing would be wrong with the child.

A couple of younger women had hurried to her, she saw Sigrid's face among them and prayed a silent prayer. The last thing she needed was to be reminded of the dead child. Both Sigrid and the dead boy had haunted her dreams at night. It wasn't death that scared her but

70

the stunning resemblance between father and son. Yes, she had seen the glances over the years and cursed herself for not being beautiful enough. The much younger Sigrid was dainty and attractive. Not as stern as she had become herself. In silence she had prayed to Freja for more beauty and to be enough for him on her own. She had borne two daughters and a son. Torvald needed another son, but she would not give him that. She was expecting a daughter. The next contraction was so strong that she fell to the ground. The child was in a hurry. She wanted to give birth lying on her side and her sister helped her hold her leg up. She braced her feet against her sister's hip. She concentrated and felt the familiar force.

Before the next contraction the nature went still, as if it was holding its breath. An aching contraction started, when it was at its peak she would push. Her breathing was shallow and quick. She waited a few seconds, quickly breathed out and in. The scream of strength echoed between the trees and bounced off the walls. She saw Sigrid put her hands over her ears. But Estrid was focused and looked deeply into her sister's eyes. On the third contraction Estrid received the child, turned onto her back and put the little one on her chest. The relief was immense.

"Get some water and linen!" the sister urged Sigrid who dreamingly lingered before she hurried away.

Estrid had already memorized the child's heavenly smell. There were no words for the great joy that rolled over her. Her hand rested on the child's small head. Had she ever felt like this before? She was filled with reverence and thankfulness. Tears ran down her cheeks. The little one was already pecking for the breast. So perfect, so complete. She felt whole without knowing that she had been half. The other hand opened the dress and let the child come to her breast.

Her sister smiled, they didn't need any more bad omens. Then her look changed. Her eyes were widened.

"Estrid", she groaned.

The sudden pain took Estrid by surprise. The last thing she saw was Sigrid's vacant face before she was lost in total darkness.

The hotel room walls gave Ann a structure to cling to. She had made the right decision not to have any clients. Her own broken phrases were the irony of faith. They were like leftovers that were beginning to stink. She picked up a half-eaten sandwich from the floor. Someone had left a banana peel on the bedside table. She had complicated her life by trying to create a reality that wasn't true. She had tried to live a life that wasn't hers. Now, the thoughts demanded to be thought. The feelings demanded a settlement! Every room she cleaned was a purge of her inner self. But she had to be careful, the thoughts always came back as if they tried to get her attention from her. Poison her. As if it were the thoughts themselves that demanded to come back to life. The thoughts created a confusion and tore her from that which she tried to find her way home to. She had to find new ways, think new thoughts, if she wanted a change in the future. She took a fumbling salsa step and thought that she would put on some music when she came home. She danced on to get clean towels from the cart in the corridor.

Eric was leaning against the doorpost. She hadn't noticed him. How long had he been standing there? She stopped but quickly decided to dance on past him. A red heat marked her cheeks. Embarrassing. Though she tried to pretend that he didn't exist.

"You seem to be in a good mood!" He smiled flirtatiously.

"Yes, don't I?" She blinked with one eye and smiled. She danced on into the toilet and hung the towels. She was done in this room. She wished Eric would let her be. Eric still stood there with his puffy old man's belly and she yet again had to push through the door opening. She pulled in her stomach and noticed that she held her breath. What was it that affected her? Why couldn't she be herself? When Eric looked at her, he made her feel cheap. Unfeminine, as if she was an object. She tried to breathe out without him hearing it. Couldn't he just move? He just stood there with his lazy glance. Had he thought that she'd danced for him?

"Alright then, I'm done and was going to lock up." She fiddled about with the keys. He didn't move until she was really close. She felt frustrated. Bullying, as if he had power over her, as if she was his private maid. She straightened herself and stared at him. She did what she always did, hid behind the mask of I-am-doing-fine-on-my-own and take-your-dirty-look-from-me attitude.

"You have to take a look at room 101. The guests have been complaining about a smell and there was some hair in the bathroom."

"Okay, I'll go there."

Without meeting his eyes, she turned her back to him and walked towards the elevator. She felt his gaze burn in her back. Her hips felt odd and her hand trembled when she pushed the elevator button. She slid into the elevator. She wanted to disappear. Hold her head in her hands and hide. Why was she ashamed? What did she have to feel ashamed of? So, she had made a couple of dance moves, but that wasn't forbidden, was it?

She felt stupid as if it was her fault that he flirted with her. Besides, he was married. She had seen his wife a few times, a middle-aged woman with her hair dyed brown. Not really good looking, but mild and good-natured in a way. Eric, on the other hand, was repulsive. With his fat body his appearance worked against him. The bald head was always shining with sweat. That was something she really didn't like about him. Then again, she had been self-employed almost her whole life. She had been able to plan her own work. She decided not to waste more energy on Eric's toad looking appearance or comments. She had enough on her own plate, and her thoughts wandered away to how stupid she'd felt when she had slipped into Samuel in her nightgown. He, who demonstratively had taken possession of the sofa the night he had uttered the word 'divorce'.

"Hey, I have to talk to you!"

"What is it? Let it be quick! I'm tired and have to sleep!"

"I'm so worried, how will it be? How will you manage in the house? With Cayla, the cooking and everything? Well, you know how she is. I've been thinking about how it could end up like this between us. I love you, Samuel! I can change. I can do things better. We can go on holidays together now that the children are older."

He sighed heavily. Turned around and said nothing.

The talking was over. Not a word. Nothing. More than twenty years and he was silent. For how long had she been standing there, listening to him breathing? She had wanted to walk up to him, caress his back. Nestle down close to him. Feel the body heat. But she didn't dare getting rejected again. How would her body hold together?

Her heart ached. Was this what they called a broken heart?

So many years together. They were an item.

A feeble voice inside of her said that it was time to get some self-respect. Let herself be formed into the woman she was. If she lived here and now without shame, she wouldn't bother about what other men or women thought. If she danced her dance and let others dance in their own way. What would life be like then?

Bibbi

Bibbi fiddled nervously with her identity card before she placed it on the desk. She had secretly booked the appointment at the gynaecologist. The fact that it was a man who met her felt shameful. What would Tobias say if he found out? She cleared her throat while she tried to tell herself that it didn't matter if she spread her legs in that horrible chair for a man or a woman, but it didn't really help.

"My genitals are hurting."

The male doctor wanted to know more. His glasses sat on the tip of his nose. She noticed that they were quite dirty and couldn't avoid wondering if it was a result of his work, from when he dived into women's private parts. Maybe his wife cleaned them for him every night. Crazy thoughts. She was nervous. It would have been easier if he asked the questions.

"It hurts after I've had sex."

"Okay?"

"It's a burning sensation. It hurts like a thousand needles."

"Have you tried using a lubricant?"

She cleared her throat again. "It's not dry or anything,

and I don't have a fungal infection."

"And how do you know that? Have you had it before?"

"This is totally different. It hurts so much that I don't know what to do. It can hurt for days."

"Contraceptives?"

"Condoms." She had tried both with and without a condom, but it hurt the same. She couldn't tell Tobias that she had the pain, because he would be angry.

"Not the pill?"

"I'm almost fifty!"

She starred absent-minded at the desk, there were a couple of forgotten coffee cups and as many papers from buns. The crumbs were spread in a childish way around the piles of papers. He must have had a cup of coffee just before she arrived. The spectacles and the crumbs gave her bad vibes. Shouldn't he have a better knowledge of her age and birth control pills? Anyone should understand that she no longer had any problems with hormones at her age, not the least a gynaecologist.

"My body has never been able to cope with the hormones", she said slowly. "I read about vulvar vestibulitis on the internet and it corresponds with what I'm experiencing."

"It seems as if you're sensitive. What does your husband say?"

"About what?"

"Condoms."

"It was my suspicion of vestibulitis that made me come here. It seems to be quite common. I would feel better if I had a name for what it is that hurts. I would feel calmer if I knew that it isn't anything dangerous."

"Well, we have to exclude the possibility of a fungal infection. Get undressed and lie down in the chair so I can take a look and see what the problem is."

"Just glide down a little bit longer. A little further!"

The chair was cold, the covering paper had slid to the side and the fake leather touched her skin. He squeezed his sausage like fingers into a pair of surgical gloves. The lubricant felt cold against her skin. Before she even had the time to think, an instrument was entering her vagina. She moaned from pain. It scraped and hurt.

"Oh, my, you're really sensitive! But it looks fine. Try some lubricant. Women in your age may need some help on the way." He patted the inside of her thighs with the moist glove before he pushed his glasses higher up on his nose.

"I'll prescribe Cipramil for your sensitivity."

She regretted that she'd come here. She felt enough shame and guilt already. It had said something about nerve pain on the internet, not about not being moist enough before sexual intercourse.

She was, but maybe not always, horny.

Ann

Ann stood still for a second before she rang on the entry phone. Charlotte had made her make the appointment. Her own first reaction was that it all was a bit hocus-pocus. Yoni massage, vaginal massage, de-armouring. Typical Charlotte things. Yet, she had turned to Mia's web site. There were things that tempted her: femininity, creative joy, healing, those words made her curious. Sex was a bustling meat market out there. But to stand vulnerable, open in her female creativity, it was something that she wished and longed for in her life. That was the reason she returned to the web site. Read on. Got information. Now she was unsure. Had she been too hasty when she made the appointment? Too influenced by Charlotte's indolence? She wanted to make sure that she had a way out and had only booked an information meeting. She inhaled heavily. Her hand shivered slightly when she pushed the button.

Dare to challenge life!

The door opened slowly, as if someone had been waiting. Ann looked in to a pair of soft green eyes. She must have looked shocked. This was not at all what she had expected when she'd been reading on the web site. The woman who met her was in her own age. About the same height. Mia had intensive green and warm eyes, just like Kevin. Small wrinkles in the corners of her eyes when she smiled. Her hair was mischievously curly, like it lived its own life. Ann giggled nervously and got sweaty under her arms. She had never done anything like this before. She'd had her own clients, not been one herself.

"Come on in, I won't bite." Mia took a step back and reached out a graceful hand to greet her. Ann was unprepared for the powerful grip, a strength that reminded her of the archetypical primitive woman. Ann could only nod as an answer and stepped into the hall. It was small and dark but cosy. There was a state of jumbled disorder. Shoes in different sizes were all over the place. The smell from cooking was lingering with a scent of Indian spice like coriander or curry. Today her thirst was unbearable and made her throat dry. Her heart was beating nervously while Mia led her into an airy room. She wore a purple dress and her hips moved concurrently with her curls. There was something free and casual about her, the same freedom as in Charlotte. Ann tried to swing her broad hips. Her shoulders were aching after all the cleaning. Would she ever be free?

"I'm used to people being nervous when they come

here. That's okay! It's part of the tension we will loosen up. Please, sit down." Mia pointed towards several scattered arm chairs. Ann had always sat in the same chair in her consulting room. Now she was panicking. Which one should she choose? She had no idea how long she stood there before she dropped down in the one closest to her.

"Do you want to sit there?"

"I don't know." She just felt small and lost.

"Do it again. Come on, stand up!"

Ann stood up and tried to relax.

"Good, stand straight in your body. Try to get in contact with the soles of your feet and close your eyes for a while. Does it feel okay?"

Ann nodded and closed her eyes. It reminded her of the yoga classes Charlotte persisted on taking her to.

"Now that you're in contact with yourself you can look up. Walk around a bit. Ask yourself where you want to sit. You can try different chairs if you want to. Where do you like it best?"

Now everything was clear to Ann. She chose a red, big wing chair. She smiled when she sat down.

"I feel at home here."

She would do it in a new way, not the old accustomed way.

"Welcome!" Mia's voice was soft but powerful. There was a presence in her eyes. She started thinking about Kevin again, there was something intimate in those eyes that made her relax when Mia smiled.

"Now your shoulders dropped from your ears!"

"Yes, but when they did that I became aware of all the other tensions in my body."

"Good."

"Good?"

"Yes, the awareness gives possibilities. To become aware is a step towards change. I consider old behavioural patterns as tensions as well. Guilt and shame are examples of what many women carry around. It's a collective inheritance. When the woman lets go of the limitations, for every blockage that is removed, she will open up for a more loving attitude to the female body."

In a light move Mia pulled her leg under her and poured two glasses of water. Ann accepted one thankfully.

"Tell me." Mia leaned forward in a reassuring manner.

"I've had an ideal image since I was a teenager. I decided not to be like my mother, who was a drunk and always had a new man. I would faithfully stay with the same man. After twenty years he wanted a divorce. I've ended up in a confusing vacuum. Anxiety and lack of sleep. My best friend says that I dwell on it. I kind of don't know what I want anymore."

"Which we noticed so well when you were going to sit down."

Ann drank the last of her water. Mia filled the glass

again as if she was familiar with the thirst.

"Yes, it's so absurd, and I've been working as an expert on relationships for the last twenty years."

A blinding sensation of getting away from a greasy infected home. A dream outside another reality. It was there I decided to become a therapist.

"I've been the classical female compromising mother. The tiger mum who grew into the role of the victim. Now I'm here and no one is thanking me for my sacrifices."

"And the tiger is roaring?"

"Exactly!"

She saw the metaphor so clearly. The tiger roared in its cage. She could hear it rattle the iron bars with its claws. It wanted to be free. In the night the tiger lay down in the cage, but as soon as she fell asleep it woke her up.

"The tiger has many good qualities. As you say, the tiger mother protects her cubs. She even drives the male away if she has to. We shall not hate and blame the men." Mia paused before she continued.

"You must learn to master the tiger. It's your inner female leader. You must find your unique expression of love and live it to the fullest."

There was something in what Mia said. The evident voice made Ann want to hear more. She took in every word, but all feelings were conflicted inside of her.

84

"My intention is to support you in your unique way of expressing love. Not because you are a loveless person, but because it's time to regain contact with your femininity, to that which is true to you today. We women have to become better to venture to be women. Even with each other."

"So far I understand you. But it's this ... vaginal massage I hesitate about."

It wasn't as difficult to say as she'd thought it would be. To her surprise, Mia laughed and the small wrinkles around her eyes became visible again. Ann felt it rub off on her. A naked giggle. A tension that loosened.

"I understand, but we do it at your own pace. If we get that far, with your permission of course, I will start by limbering up your belly with circulating moves to get rid of the tension. Like massage. We establish trust to each other, a teamwork that is based on what you want. You will always have a choice and I'm here to support you. Nothing says it has to be vaginal."

"I had so many questions before I came here, but now they're all gone."

"This is how I feel: we women communicate without words. Your questions are answered by my presence. When you take part of my consciousness. Or if it's even my consciousness? I think that we're more influenced by each other than science will ever be able to prove."

It was with a comfortable feeling Ann left. Mia had given her a hug. A friendly hug, like an old friend. It felt like they already knew one another. She both wanted and didn't want to make a new appointment. Self-respect and her own value were something that had sunk into her. Something inside of her tempted her to transform. At the same time, it felt too intimate. Another person so close. And a woman. She'd been given a question to take home with her.

Who am I free to live my female expression?

During the days that followed, the thoughts continued to haunt Ann. Why had she contacted Mia? Would massaging her stomach really make her feel better? She'd also been stupid and contacted Samuel again about the division of the joint property of husband and wife. He was angry and brusque. Not a shred of cooperation. The nights were filled with a mist av thoughts and a haze of dreams. The lack of sleep consumed her. Her body was aching. Her focus swung, and she got a feeling of not really being there. She bumped into things or just dropped what she held in her hands.

A light rain wet her down on her way home from the hotel. It had been a busy day. Eric had been flirting and following her. Why did she feel such aversion to his looks?

The tiger roared in its cage. She cooled down by letting the rain trickle over her face. Her legs drove her home. She didn't like to confess it, but she was once again in a paralysed state almost immediately after meeting Mia. Shouldn't it be the other way around? She experienced herself as a bystander watching her own life, like from above. She'd read that it could happen after severe shock or trauma. She had hoped that Mia would suggest a direction,

a goal somewhere there in the fog. The imprint on her ongoing emotional journey was bitter and tiresome. A bitter
lemon. And she was well aware that it was her and nobody
else that had to let go of that bitter lemon.

It was the 'tone' she needed to change. The vibra-
tion that would guide her to another path in the future.
She would write her own notes. What did her unique tone
sound like? Had she ever been aware of it?

Once at home and soaking wet she put on a wool
sweater. She was shivering. She sat down on the sofa with
a blanket over her legs. The water was trickling down the
window and pattered on the windowsill. She closed her
eyes. The sound made her relax. It reminded her of the
summer house, her cottage. She could easily see the image before her. Smell the scent. A small house in the archipelago. Every little angle was so familiar. The stone stairs,
every little patch of grass was imprinted in her cells. The
flat rock that met the water. A little seaweed that swung in
the waves. A few reeds that had blown in with the waves.
She felt the splinters on the wooden jetty and the sea licking
her body. The children splashing on a rainy day. Muddy
feet. She loved to be there, all the experiences that had been
collected in her and had become a part of her. Familiar and
like home. A tone that she liked.

88

Bibbi

Bibbi's restlessness drove her to stay a couple of extra hours in the gym. It was the only thing that helped her with her thoughts. It was buzzing like a bee hive in her head. Yesterday's failure made her go over the same things over and over again. What had happened to everything that was good? Their relationship was sometimes in chaos. No matter how she tried, it was always her fault, she who misinterpreted things. Exaggerated. Made a mountain out of a molehill. But she had seen the message. 'I love you', and a heart. She had heard the pling and looked down at his telephone. He had said it was from a customer. "What? It's nothing!"

It wasn't the first time. The schism made her feel sick. His words made her want to throw up. The sweat ran down her back and the stair climber continued persistently. Her legs felt heavy and the lactide acid built up in her legs and almost killed her, but she knew that she had to push herself more if she wanted peace of mind. He used to appreciate her the way she was. Bring her gifts. It had been that way in the beginning. He had even said it: "I am going to do this sometimes, give you presents." It was alluring lingerie in black or red lace. She liked it when he looked at her with appreciation. When he wanted her. That look had changed to a possessive gaze that she didn't feel comfortable with. As if she would always stay by his side, no matter what he did. She'd tried to change to please him. She had always taken him back to what she thought was love. But when had love turned in to empty promises?

He was unfaithful!

He didn't notice her any more. Ignored her. She moved around unnoticed, like a ghost in their home. He kept quiet when she asked questions that he thought were uncalled for. He didn't think it was any of her business. She'd recently put on the sexy underwear and he had called her a lesbian. She'd felt sad and cheap. But later he'd said that it was a *nice* word to him, that he only said it to beautiful women. But she knew all too well which ones that were lesbians to him. The tears burnt behind her eye lids. She stepped on. The machine was revving fast. Her irritation was turning into anger and she switched to the tread mill. She had to talk to him, explain how she felt! Make him understand!

No text messages, no missed phone calls. Had she gone too far this time? Would he leave her? The panic grew. She didn't know what feeling it was that filled her so that her chest ached. After a long shower Bibbi decided to visit him at the office.

She stopped outside the door. She wet her lips. Focused

90

on her breathing. Tried to imagine how he went to the door. She'd been working out hard at the gym. The small of her back was aching. What was it the body therapist had said about back pains? That she lacked support in her life. She pushed the thought aside. She must keep herself together now. She straightened her skirt. Felt naked. Did she dress too provocative? He didn't like it when she showed up with too little on among other people. All of a sudden, she felt old. Adult. Inside, her body tingled nervously. Tensed. The door handle was pulled down and he gave her space to come in. Her eyes got caught in his and when he opened up his arms she sank into his embrace. His strong arms around her. She sunk deeper into his hug. His scent was nice and mixed with a touch of male deodorant. The manly, so familiar, strong forearms that held her, took good care of her. She didn't know how long they stood there but the stillness and the closeness made her calm. She didn't want to lose him!

"It's nice to see you, darling!"

She had a feeling that he meant it. But what about what had happened yesterday? The harsh words he'd said? Had he meant them?

"I would like some water." The thirst reminded her. Or was it just an escape to get some time?

"Come." He took her hand and led her to the office kitchenette and poured her a glass of water.

She drank it all. He pulled her to him again. They came

closer. The smell again. Did he feel the same as she did? Both times it had been him who started the embrace. One of his arms slowly slid over her back up towards her neck. She shivered. A longing for what used to be. She hadn't dared to dream of a welcome like this. Was it possible that she'd dramatized everything yesterday, had made it all up in her limited world of feelings? All she wanted was that they met in a mutual vision.

Open.

Faithful.

Belonging.

She must have imagined it. The thoughts of infidelity must be her fabrication, just like he'd always said. She breathed out and sunk deeper into his hug. She would focus on that she wished for in life. His hand stroke her back. The muffled sound from the cars outside, somewhere she thought she heard an ambulance. Life was really too short. Of course, it was the two of them. She had been so stupid.

His hand searched its way up to the nape of her neck. The bare skin on his fingertips made her react. She enjoyed the touch. Small, pleasantly shivers. She gently pressed against him to show that she appreciated his hand. His grip around her got tighter. Kind of squeezed her neck, he carefully pulled up the thin sweater with his other hand. She felt passive, let him take initiative. Her thoughts floated away. All the words she'd planned to say, the feelings she'd decided to try to explain, were dissolved. Her lower parts were pulsating, her breasts ached under his hand. She felt how he got harder inside his jeans. She parted her legs, pressed up against him. She enjoyed the feeling of being someone to him. That he wanted her there and now. Only the now existed. She felt complete together with him.

She felt sexy. He tasted good, a little salt. Maybe something he had eaten.

"I want you!"

He swept her up, carried her lightly. She fitted so well in his arms. She took in his smell. It felt so natural to be carried, as if she would always be his. He carefully lay her down on the desk. Looked at her the way she'd always wanted to be seen. She felt so beautiful. Wanted. Full of expectation.

What was he going to do with her?

"You drive me crazy!"

His words vibrated between them. It meant orgasm. Was that what she wanted? She still felt hurt. Deep in her chest the injustice was burning, a feeling that she wasn't good enough, didn't measure up to his expectations. He sent loving text messages to others behind her back. That hurt.

"You ..." She let her hand caress his hair. She wanted him to understand that it was his behaviour that had hurt her, not him.

He bent down over her. Found her lips again. His tongue searched hungrily over her teeth.

"You are so beautiful, Bibbi, everything about you is beautiful."

He looked deep into her eyes and then let his gaze glide over her breasts. He pulled her sweater up. Took one of her breasts in his hand. Teased her nipple till it got stiff. She liked it when he looked at her. That look made her feel beautiful, as if she was the only one to him. She would never get enough of it. She was always his. She must devote herself to him, so he would stay with her forever. She tried to enjoy it, but the desk galled her skin and she hadn't forgot about the pain afterwards. The thought that she maybe wasn't the first on his desk made her body slowly react. Her genitals got dry. She tried to move rhythmically. Rubbed her feminine parts against him. Her underwear came off. He pushed two fingers inside of her. His nails chafed against the sensitive skin. She faked an orgasm.

"Now it's my turn."

She looked at him like she'd almost forgot that he was there. His hair was sweaty. She felt done. Didn't want to. He pulled her off the table to a standing position, and with a firm grip he turned her around and placed her hands on the desktop. With experienced hands he pressed his cock into her. She got tense. It hurt. She'd never liked it from behind. He held her and moved her back and forth. Her body was still tired from the hard work out. The hard and rhythmical thrusts hit against her womb and she bit hard in her lip to avoid crying.

94

Ann

Charlotte raised an eyebrow. She thought Ann was a coward.

”At least you can go there for another meeting!”

”Yes, maybe”, Ann sighed. There was something alluring with Mia, yet she made her unbearably nervous. She had that gaze that saw right through you, like you couldn’t hide. Whatever it was she was hiding from. Herself?

”What are you afraid of?”

”Afraid? Me? What do you mean?”

Charlotte knew what trigged her.

Today Mia wore a green dress when she opened the door. Her hair was even curlier, and the apartment smelled of other spices. Her hips swayed as easy and graceful as last time. Ann followed her and tried to make her own hips sway. She just wanted to talk, and Mia had said that it was okay.

”What do you like to do?”

”I don’t know!” The question surprised Ann.

”You probably know what you don’t like. Do you like cooking? Baking?”

"I don't know. I used to, or I thought I did. I liked it when the whole family was gathered around the table." Her throat was choking. The tears came. Charlotte would have been disappointed if she'd seen her now. Ann bit the inside of her cheek.

"We always had dinner at five thirty and gathered around the table."

"Put your hand over your womb. You can close your eyes if you want to. Share what's on your mind."

The wind is lashing outside the window, the autumn has arrived with full force. A storm warning has been issued. It's November and the kind of day when the sun never shines. It's five thirty in the evening and everyone is gathered in the kitchen at Winding Road. Samuel smiles and listens intently to the children. I look at him and I feel proud. Beside him I feel complete. My whole family is gathered. Simon is five and Cayla is three years old. We're happy that there will be chocolate mousse for dessert and laughing at the fact that it looks like poop. It's a Saturday evening. The storm howls outside and it is cosy to be indoors. I have everything I need. He has bought some wine. An expensive good tasting wine. I have bought cheese and grapes. We like it this way. It feels luxurious. Our wonderful family. The nice house. We hold each other's gaze for a long time. I press my leg against his. The tension's in the air, and as soon as the kids are in front of the tv, we start touching each other. It's like we're newly in love. I must be the luckiest woman in the world, that's how it feels. I feel fortunate.

The children are asleep. We make out on the sofa. He starts caressing me. Glides down the inside of my thigh. God, how I want him. He teases me. It all goes so fast. Do I dare ask him to take it slower? I want to enjoy this, let it take its time. Receive it in full. We have all night.

Suddenly he stands up.

Has he noticed my thoughts and interpret them as a rejection? I hold out my hand to show him that I want him.

"You make me crazy! I must have you now!"

He mumbles something about protection and starts to walk away.

"No, don't go! I want you now! Come, I want to!"

Don't leave me, my body says. We can snuggle afterwards.

"Are you not ovulating?"

"No, no. Take me! How do you want me?"

I must have him close. My body cannot make it without him. We belong together. Without each other we are split. He is hard when he penetrates me. It hurts a little. I wasn't really ready to let him come inside of me. The fear of being left alone forces me to not say anything. I bite my cheek to hold back my tears. He doesn't like it if I cry. The cheeses are untouched on the table.

Everything is perfect in my life. We belong together. We're just one. Our bodies are lying still on the sofa. His

hand is still around my breast. The sofa from Ikea. Our naked bodies. Mixed body fluids trickle out on the cushion. It
can be washed. I lay still and listen to his familiar breathing.
I am filled. Wide-awake. He falls quickly asleep. It doesn't
matter. I feel loved. Acknowledged. Whole as a woman and
I sneak upstairs, take a look at the children and get a quilt.
I tuck him in. I feel such satisfaction in my body. I smile. A
quick glance in the mirror. My cheeks are rosy and my eyes
sparkle.

It took hardly two weeks before I understood that I was
pregnant. My whole body rejoiced. The days that followed
were euphoric. I'm going to be a mother again. I smile at
my children. They smile at me. I smile at the world, it smiles
back. Don't I feel a bit of morning sickness? Maybe a little,
but that doesn't matter. Nothing in the whole world can
take anything from me. Never. True happiness. I cannot
wait until my bump will show. I will surprise him, let him
see it with his own eyes. Not tell him yet, but let it be a
pleasant surprise. I dress extra nice. Put on some make-up.
I smile so much that it almost hurts. He's absent-minded at
the dinner table. I wait until the children are asleep. He's
already in bed. My husband. The man I love. The man
I've chosen as a life companion. He reads one of his many
crime novels to fall asleep.

"Hey", I say and follow the bridge of his nose with my
forefinger.

"Hm, not right now. I'm almost falling asleep."

I bite my cheek nervously. I want to share my happiness with him. His words make me sad. Hormones already? I pull my finger abruptly from him and he turns to me.

”Okay, what is it?”

”We’re having another baby. I am pregnant!”

”What the hell?” He sits upp quickly, supporting himself with his forearms. ”I did think about it because of the way you walk around and smile and act.”

”Act?”

”You must understand that we can’t have another child. Two is enough. I’ve said so! Don’t you get it, we can’t have three children. Damn! Was it necessary to bring it up right now? I have to get up early to go to work tomorrow!”

He turns away. Pulls the cover over himself. The book falls to the floor.

Nothing more.

Not a word.

I lie still in the dark. Stare at the ceiling. At times the light reflects from a car through the gap in the blind. Hand on my stomach. Eighth week. He doesn’t want it. Doesn’t want it. The mantra fills me. I don’t know what to do with myself. He, the love of my life, doesn’t want to have a child with me. After several hours I take my pillow and sneak down next to Simon. I take his hand. It’s already getting lighter when I finally fall asleep.

Mia hands her several paper-napkins. Ann nods and accepts them. It’s nice when she lets go, but all the crying makes her sound nasal. She hasn't told anyone, not even Charlotte, but now the words are pouring out of her.

He stood next to me when I felt something let go. Now there was no turning back. The life that died in me. I sank down to the floor. He became worried, got hold of me and tried to pull me to my feet. He was frowning. I wouldn't accept his help, I would show him that I could cope without him. He tried to support me on the way to the toilette.

"Does it hurt a lot?"

"Go!" My voice had a shrill, high-pitched tone that I didn't recognize. He stopped, surprised.

"Go away!"

He cautiously backed out through the door. I quickly locked it and sat down on the toilet seat. I could hear him outside. I wanted to be alone. I was bleeding heavily. I didn't dare think of what it would look like in the toilet. Maybe there was a foetus floating down there. A life that I had agreed to kill. How would I ever be able to forgive myself? There was a pressure in my head. They had two children together, didn't they have enough love for three? It hurt. I'd forgotten to take those two pain killers that was part of the Murder plan.

I doubled with my hands on my stomach and staggered from the bathroom to the bedroom. I had never felt so alone in my whole life. Samuel sat on the stairs outside and smoked. He only smoked when he was extremely tense, like before a flight or a big presentation. He'd taken the day off. We had decided that.

He was supposed to support her. Relieve her of getting the children from school. On the third day everything would hopefully be painlessly over. Take the pain killers, they'd said.

The pain in my soul was endless. All happiness was gone. I returned to the bathroom and threw up. There were still some drops of blood on the seat. I wiped it off with toilet paper. That was all that was left, small drops. My baby. I sobbed. How could I ever forgive myself? I took a long warm shower. We had run out of soap. The stairs to the bedroom felt endless. The bed was soaked in sunlight. The clock showed 11:11, the same time that Cayla was born. A stab in my womb. I took two pain killers. Pulled down the blind. I would sleep it all off. One word echoed in my head. The word grew inside to a disastrous migraine like an explosion.

It was dark when he came up. I could hear the children play downstairs. He smelled of a mix of toothpaste and smoke. He sat down on the side of the bed. I lay still. Something inside of me had died, it had followed the blood in the toilet.

"Darling!"

He took her cold hand. Yes, she was dying. His warmth touched her now. Tears started to trickle down her cheeks. There was a long silence. A water pump had started, and the radiators clicked. Otherwise it was quiet. One could sense the life outside. A car honked far away. The neighbour's dog barked. A totally normal week night that was palpable outside.

"My darling!"

Samuel's voice was low. I could hear that he'd been crying. I could be able to forgive him, but it would be difficult to forgive myself. Impossible.

I took his hand. He stroked my hair. He looked at me in the dark. We went through this together. Everything would be as usual again. Just a few days, not more than a week, then it all would be like before, I told myself. Our wonderful family.

I threw myself in his arms. It was the two of them forever.

A month later, I went up to the attic. Cleared out all the baby toys and all tiny clothes and drove everything to the charity shop. It was the two of them forever, them and their two children. I'd been so stupid to think otherwise.

Mia holds her hand. It feels safe. Manicured, short nails. Mia doesn't try to correct her. There's no right or wrong in her story. She just looks warmly at her with understanding. She knows. Ann looks around in the room. What had happened couldn't be changed.

"I miss what could have been!"

The train goes faster. It's cold. The snow whirls around it. She looks down at the high healed stilettoes that are stuck in the rail. She pulls her foot but the cold makes it hard. A rose bay stands in the snow. It's cold. Very cold. The train shrieks on its way. The eyes of the engine stares at her. She cannot move. There is no chance to flee. It's too late. The train moves alarmingly closer. She stares at the rose bay; the black heals against the soft powder snow. The paralysis drains her and the fear takes over. She knows exactly what will happen. Yet, she does nothing. Now it splits her in two. The blood splashes. Splashes up on the windows. She watches the train that looks like a black snake that wriggles away. The stilettoes on one side of the rail, on the other side the rose bay sleeps quietly against the bloodstained snow. She tries to wipe the blood away with a piece of toilet paper.

She wakes up soaked in sweat. The room is dark, and she fumbles for her phone. The terror upsets her.

What if fear is a perception of danger.
Has something happened to the children? She sits up and closes her eyes. Her heart is still thumping. Simon? Cayla?

Only the beat of her heart breaks the silence. The recurring train that splits her. The blood on the snow.

All of a sudden, she is wide awake. She won't flee, not hide. If she wants to be free, she has to explore every part from the inside. She breathes in the fear. A curiosity that she hasn't felt in a long time immediately appears. Something new before her. She felt it as a child. She felt it during the first period in the house with Samuel. An exploring tingle as if a new adventure was waiting around the corner. The subtle smell of something new. If she listened carefully, she could hear how the energy flowed in her body. It was a bit frightening to hear the blood run through her veins, feel the heartbeat. From the inside. She'd been living in a vacuum, a compromised life, a package. She had not been living as the person she was meant to be.

If she listened, she could hear her tone. A vague vibrating sound of all the sounds together in her body. For how long did she sit there? Listening in the presence.

When she opened her eyes, it had become light in the room. For the first time in a long time she could feel that she was deeply rooted in her body. As if it had an extra skin or a shell that held everything in place. She let her hand glide over her arm. She felt the touch from her palm, the surface of her body, but also the inside of it. She'd never experienced anything like it. As if she was in her body but at the same time the person who experienced it. She wanted to stay. Just stay in this being. If she moved, she might lose that which she'd just found. But the tingle in her body enticed a movement of doing. She got up. Stretched. She felt. She lived. A conscious feeling of *I am*.

The birds made more noise than usual. The spring was here to stay. The tingling hummed like a bumble-bee in her body when she hurried to the shop. She glanced at her watch, they had just opened. The exploring had made her hungry. Her stomach felt empty and she was longing for avocado, bread and a nice cheese. She would buy soy milk and make a cappuccino. She carried home two full bags. She made coffee and filled a tray. She made it so cosy and it felt so natural. She got the quilt from the bed and put it on the leather sofa. She was going to get the rug from Winding Road, then she would be spared from the cold leather. This place could be really cosy. She looked around. She could get some new things, make it her own home. She wanted to let the light in. The windows were fantastic. There was potential. She would start by writing an e-mail to her landlord and ask if she could put some things in the attic. Maybe she would even contact Samuel today and arrange a meeting. In a neutral place. A place that they never used to go to. She would ask if she could get her things from the house. She would write a list of what was important to her, that was part of her life.

She started with the hall, the first room that met you when you came in. Bucket and a swab. The high ceiling had to be shown, she thought. If she could hang a rectangular painting where the mirror was and move that to the short side by the door. She moved one of the plastic plants from the bedroom to the hall. She hadn't liked it. Now it looked quite good. Who knew there was a place for everything in life? Now she moved the heavy furniture around, moved a small side table where she could put her keys and the mail. Took down the hatrack with a kitchen-knife. Instead she would use the wardrobe for the coats. Time disappeared.

She had a plan. Made lists. One for Samuel. A list of things to get from Winding Road. A list of things to buy. She would move in to the apartment. A home. She hadn't even called it a home before, just seen it as a halt. But her body wanted it to be homely. She went on until it got dark outside. The bedroom, bathroom and kitchen. Now there was only the living room left. The curtains had been taken down, they would also end up in a box in the attic. She'd got an okay from the landlord. There were more things to carry up. She liked using her body like this. Her stiff muscles started to soften, and the sweat was sticky on her back. She played music and the hours flew by. She would ask Simon to help her with the heaviest things. Maybe his friend Kevin, with the dark eyes, could come with him. She didn't feel ashamed that she thought he was good looking. Not today. Attractive and beautiful was one thing, to go to bed was something else. She'd been texting with Charlotte during the day, getting encouraging words. Tomorrow she would go on with her new life. Her body felt so light.

Oh, a missed call from her mother. At once the guilt hit her and made her unable to act.

But wait:
Was it really her guilt?
Who am I who is free of guilt?
Who am I as a woman without guilt?

"Hi, Mum!"

"So, you're calling now. Haven't you seen that I called?" The sharp, raucous voice that witnessed of a life with a lot of alcohol, made her automatically pull the phone from her ear. She turned down the volume. She saw the big jaws of guilt that would easily get hold of her. But not today. She was determined now.

I hear you!

"How do you think it feels to sit here all by myself?"

You are my mother!

"Hasn't Samuel called you?"

"No, should he?"

"Haven't you heard? Cayla has fallen off a horse!"

A sharp tug in her stomach, a knot of worry started to bounce around like a ping-pong ball in her stomach. The

sound of a speeding train got higher in her head. She started to breathe heavily. The images of an ambulance and a
bleeding Cayla was displayed before her eyes. The dream.
The blood. A bad sign.

”What happened?” Her voice got another tone and she
was already on her way to the door. She had to take a taxi
to the hospital.

”I can’t believe that you haven’t spoken to Samuel! You
two really have to solve this for the sake of your children!”

And that should come from her!

”But what has happened? Please, Mum, where’s Cayla?”

”They should be on their way home now. You two are
not talking to each other. Don’t you understand how this
affects the children? By the way, what will happen to the
summer party?”

”On their way home?”

”Yes, I guess it was a sprain or a dislocation. Don’t you
speak with your own children either? Don’t you call them?”

”Mum, I will call now and find out what has happened.” The table tennis ball bounces less and the images
of the ambulance was replaced by Samuel and Cayla on
their way home in the polished car.

She exhaled a couple of times and established the fact
that she made a partly successful attempt to keep the guilt
away in an emergency situation.

Cayla's mobile phone was turned off. When was the last time that happened?

Samuel answered after the first signal.

"Hi, what's happened?"

"Everything's under control."

He sounded tense. Yet, she was surprised by how nice it felt to hear his voice.

"What's happened to Cayla?"

"It's all good now."

She'd have to drag it out of him.

"Can I speak to her?"

"She's in the shower now, but I'll tell her that you called.

"Great, thanks. We should meet and go through our finances. Do you have a time that suits you?" Sweat was starting to seep in the palm of her hand and she suddenly became aware that she must stink of sweat after moving around the furniture. This was all new to her: not being able to take care of Cayla. Having to book a meeting and agree on their finances. Hear his distance.

"I can text you some suggestions."

In the shower she went through her conversation with her mother again. Would she be able to invite people to the annual summer party? What would Samuel say about that? He could easily say no if it didn't suit him. Kevin and Simon. Cayla. The summer neighbours Tobias and Bibbi. Charlotte and the others? Her mum and David. The usual gang. The questions were many. Would they even keep the summer house? She let the water run over her and her shoulders sunk. Live there, she hadn't thought about it. She felt at home there. It had been an eventful day. Notes started to take shape.

Samuel

Samuel looked at her with that little anxious glance. He let it linger and studied her from head to toe. Something bothered him. She had changed. She looked complacent. A hatred spread in him. How could she, after all those years that she'd been living off of him? He'd been carrying the heavy financial load when the children had been growing up. Taken care of the children, as it was so nicely put. He pulled his hand through his hair. He hadn't been prepared for this. He'd seen her before his eyes; pale with the grey hair untidy and a sweater that hid her breasts. Begging, a bit slouched forward begging for money. Instead he had a secure woman in front of him. In good shape and with a healthy colour in her face. Tight jeans and a jacket. Weren't those jeans a little too provocative? One could see the hips and how they stretched over her bottom. A thrill rushed through his body. He knew her smell and how she felt down there. She'd been his. He squirmed a little. Felt uncomfortable. The last months had been tough. He'd had a fling just to damp down the feeling that he was inadequate. But that woman was younger and lacked something that he couldn't put his finger on. It was obvious that she sucked in her belly and pouted with her breasts and that her moaning wasn't genuine. He now realized that he missed their family life, longed for what Ann and he had had together. That bothered him. Her change made him feel like a failure. Who was Ann seeing? Who made her blossom? His curious eyes locked automatically in the cleavage between her breasts. An image flashed by of when she breastfed Simon. The warmth from her rounded bosom. She was his.

Ann held out her hand to greet him. The feelings were confusing. A handshake after all these years? Weren't they going to hug? He felt totally unprepared. He wanted to hug her, feel her against him. The warmth. A picture of her, standing on all four as she took a man's stiff shaft inside her passed by. How she moaned for real, a genuine moan when the man filled her. He cleared his throat. Quickly took her hand. It was so soft, so strong. He cleared his throat again. Let go of her hand a little too hasty. He saw her questioning glance. They knew each other. Knew each other's faces. He nodded to her to sit down. He needed to gather himself. Think business-like. Leave the feelings behind.

To feel is not the same as feelings.

They ordered mineral water. He'd meant to buy her lunch, but she was quick to say that they wanted to split the bill. Meanwhile he decided to brace himself, put all feelings aside. But the images of Ann and another man kept trying to appear before his eyes. She must have met someone! He would ask Cayla and Simon to look into it.

He had prepared all the papers and already arranged to get their signatures witnessed. He presented his suggestions in a professional manner and placed the division of the joint property and the premarital settlement on the table. She asked for a possibility to read it through at home in peace and quiet. It was then he lost it.

"In peace and quiet?" He was on his way to stand up. She sat as if nothing had happened. He felt the contempt grow. Wouldn't she even be satisfied with this after all these years? What was she thinking?

He leaned forward and hissed: "What else do you think you'll get? I'm actually the one who earned the money."

Ann calmly unfolded a piece of paper from her handbag.

"I would like to get this from the house, or if you rather put it all together and let me know when I can collect it."

She placed the paper in front of him. Her calm manner annoyed him. He wanted to yell at her. That, which bothered him the most, was her sexual appeal. As if she thought that she was something special. A bloody fifty-year old woman. She'd always been such a know-all. He glanced through the list of things. He saw no problems with it but couldn't just nod and say okay. A little more resistance would probably make her lose her track.

"So, you think you have the right to all of this?" His voice was tense, and he cleared his throat several times.

"Yes, please!"

"Yes, please? You just sit there like a yes-woman."

"You know, Samuel. I thought we could handle this like adults!"

She was ready to stand up. He took her wrist. She looked at him. He couldn't read her look. Contempt or goodness? He didn't know anymore! He didn't recognize her. He'd lost her. He tried not to sound so desperate.

"Sit down, okay!"

She calmly stood still.

"I'm done. Let me know when everything can be picked up! I don't think the smaller things have to be part of the documented division of our joint property since you get to keep the rest. I'll get back to you when I've read the documents."

She twisted her hand from his grip with surprising strength and left.

Whore, bloody whore!

He refused to look after her. But he could feel her hips move. She had freed herself from him and the family. Didn't they mean anything to her anymore?

Bloody lesbian!

114

Bibbi

The morning pee. A minute of waiting, a stick with 99% certainty. Her first reaction when the line appeared was to call someone. The other pleasantly confirmed that her nausea was due to hormones. There was a proof. The third was a worry over how Tobias would react. He had mentioned that he wasn't very fond of children and didn't want to commit in that way. Tobias argued with her. Her old friends ganged up on her and thought that Tobias had bad influence over her.

Think about what you're doing!

The midwife advised her not to wait too long to tell him.

"Cook a nice dinner, something extra nice and tell him. It gets harder the longer you wait." She had encouraged her to devote herself to the relationship.

The morning sickness possessed her, and the thoughts of if she really wanted to have the baby interchanged with images of her happily walking with the pram. Tobias walked beside her. He would be such a loving father.

Tobias was impatient at home and the days passed before she told him. Mildly put there were mood swings. She tried to calm down with household chores. Dare to show her feelings. Indulge in the relationship.

It was now it was going to happen, Friday afternoon. She had treated herself to flowers from the florist. A romantic bouquet, she'd told the shop assistant. The walk home was light. She saw prams everywhere. She smiled. A nice feeling of finally being able to tell Tobias. She didn't have exclusive rights to her stomach. It belonged to them both. She'd planned it in her thoughts and even rehearsed what to say in front of the mirror. If she put her hand on the stomach, she could feel a swelling. A tiny hard, round ball. She'd looked up food recipes for a couple of weeks. She'd tried to think of how he felt and how she could make him feel more comfortable. Dinner was on the table, it had taken her all day to prepare it. She'd read the recipe several times. Her upbringing was characterized by easy cooked dishes. Food you could take straight from the stove. Over cooked sausages that bobbed in greasy water. Dry fish fingers that had been too long in the freezer. Black pudding. Her mother had her exciting news, and then it could be sliced Chinese leaves with oranges. She shuddered. No wonder she had become a health freak. She was not at all as good at cooking as Tobias was, but felt domestic and handy. She would probably like being a mother. She could learn. This, to prepare, set the table and make it look good, was also all new to her. Just like affording fresh flowers on the table. She felt satisfied.

”What kind of soup is this?”

”The sauce?”

”Yes, is it a joke, or what?”

”No, I thought you’d like it.” The tears stung behind her eyes. She had done her best.

”You must understand that I can’t eat this watery sauce to my steak. Look, it just leaks through the fork. What were you thinking?”

He let the sauce run through the prongs of the fork.

”I don’t think.” Bibbi looked down on her plate, but really, she saw through it, under the table and stopped on her belly. Something was growing inside of there. A lump that would form to a life. She had also been a lump in a stomach. It couldn’t be like it had been for her, an unwelcomed life. A living, indefinable lump the parents weren’t able to love.

It became too much. Tobias’ reaction. The shame over not having said anything. The sauce she thought she’d manage to make but wasn’t good enough. Fresh flowers that got pale. In her exposure she ran into the bedroom and slammed the door. She lay down and sobbed. Old tears welled up, everything that she had held inside herself for such a long time. The door remained closed and it was all silent outside. If he only could come in and hold her, but the door stayed shut and she fell asleep.

Bibbi got a sick note for depression from the doctor.

Ann couldn't control her fingers, they seemed to live their own floundering life now. But she managed to call Charlotte, who answered right away.

"How did it go?"

"He was angry, tried to frame me in a strange way."

"Shall we meet? It sounds like you need some moral support."

"Yes, please. I'm shaking."

Charlotte whistled when she saw Ann.

"Hello, gorgeous!" Charlotte held her at arm's length.

"So sexy, and sensual!"

"Thanks, you're so sweet!" The compliment warmed her. That was how she felt. Now that she was freer in her body.

"You will surely meet someone soon. I promise!" Charlotte blinked and sat down at the open-air restaurant.

She was still only thirsty for water, but Charlotte always had the effect on her that it was okay to drink wine in the middle of the week.

"Come on. Let's share a bottle, I'm buying. We have something to celebrate!"

"We do? What?"

"Yes, you as a free woman!"

Ann laughed out loud and leaned forward, swung with her hair just like free women do. In a short version she told about Samuel. Charlotte listened intently.

"You know, Samuel understands that he has no power over you. Men do that, they try to have power over the woman. Possessiveness. You will notice the difference now that you are no longer a victim."

"A victim?"

"Yes, you are no longer a victim! Financially independent and free in your own body. Tell me you have caressed your breasts as I told you to?" Charlottes eyes were smiling.

"Not really."

Ann smiled back. She knew that she had more to explore about her body. She had just begun to find her way back to it as a woman. For the first time in her life she thought it was okay to look at herself in the mirror.

"Let's talk about the future. Samuel is a closed chapter." She was surprised by her own frankness, yet she had a fragment before her eyes: the picture of when she stood up, and he with a hiss had spat out the words. The hatred in his eyes. Twenty-two years. All the feelings that had come and left.

Ann stayed and sipped her wine a long while after Charlotte had gone. Comfortable thoughts of what they had talked about, holidays and the future. With small, small steps she moved on and now she had definitely come so far that she saw there had been a change. Charlotte gave her support. Mia stood behind her as a safe haven. Samuel's outburst had made her stand up to him even though it had been shaky. She hadn't backed down. She knew his life strategy. Power was close at hand to him. She mustn't forget that she was the one who'd accepted that behaviour. Deeply rooted needs of satisfying the family peace. She'd spoken a lot about it with Charlotte. About how it was to grow up in a dysfunctional family and a single mother who was an alcoholic. Men that passed by. Unfulfilled needs as a child. The pursuit of confirmation; she had sold herself out. We women must become better at keeping our self–respect and self-esteem, Charlotte had said.

She looked at other people. They looked so happy. Laughed without worries. Sun and blue sky. It was her life too. Cayla had called yesterday, bubbling over. Told her about the horse riding, unhampered. She wanted them to meet soon. Maybe go to the movies. A mother–daughter-day as she called it. And Simon's sweet texts that always ended with hearts. Kevin had said hello. And she had friends, that was too easy to forget. Charlotte. She could talk about anything with her. And the girls, even if she felt a bit odd in their shallowness, they were still her friends. Even the girls at work started to treat her as a friend. They cared about each other and if someone wasn't there, they missed her. She had switched shifts with Maija today, a young girl who'd wished her good luck. She longed to the hotel and home. Her new life. Soon, all her things would be in place. The apartment had got a makeover, as Simon had called it. He and Kevin had showed up one night and she'd felt more relaxed than ever. She even had been barefoot in a short skirt and a tank top. Without a bra. That was how free she felt. Summery. The thoughts of living in the country in the summer cottage started to take shape. The thought that went on in the background even though she hadn't told anyone.

With conflicting feelings, she started to walk home. A vague gnawing feeling of emptiness had turned up. Everyone else seemed so happy hand in hand. Someone to love. Here she walked all alone. Her good self-esteem was fading. Samuel's irritated look showed up time after time. She faltered but wasn't going to give up. She took the long way home. Walked along new streets she'd never been to before. Looked up at new house fronts. Tried to convince herself that life was wonderful. The evening sun warmed her, and the world smiled. It was the contrasts that formed life. Just a year ago everything had been as usual. A tug in her heart when she thought of the summer cottage, her retreat. Her real home. She'd hardly given it a thought, just been occupied by feelings. It hurt to think about selling it, the thought of going there was an even greater pain.

"It's time to leave the old behind", Charlotte had whispered.

Create that new, find your way back to yourself. She shouldn't hope that Samuel would cooperate. If she put all her expectations behind her, she wouldn't have to meet more disappointments and betrayals. She'd just got in when she heard a quiet knock. She opened the door slightly.

"Kevin?" Ann exasperated. She must have looked surprised.

"Hi, I saw you and followed you, but you didn't hear me."

"Oh, hi." She took an awkward step back and let him in.

He held out his hand, a firm handshake. With the other hand he pushed the sunglasses to his forehead. His eyes were intense, just as she remembered them. Her cheeks blushed and reminded her of the intimate fantasies she'd had. She felt the warmth from his hand, it infused security. He took a step closer and at first, she thought that he would give her a hug, but he just held her hand for a while.

"I'd love to come in for a while, there's something I want to talk to you about." He bent down to take off his shoes.

"Yes, of course!" Ann snuck into the bathroom. She tidied herself up and let the cold water run over her wrists. The thoughts started again. So, Kevin felt the same as she. He wanted to talk about something. She cursed herself for drinking wine. The spots of sweat had dried, and she put on some deodorant in her armpits and toothpaste in her mouth. She didn't want to stay too long in the bathroom but needed some me-time. How would she get out of this? What did she want? Her body wanted one thing. Curl up in his arms and surrender to his kisses. He was the same age as her son. Be real Ann, she tried to tell herself while she fixed her hair and straightened her back.

He waited in the sofa. The sun shone with its last rays and created a romantic soft summer light in the living room.

"Sit here." Kevin made room for her in the sofa. She liked that he asked her. Told her with a soft certainty that witnessed of what he wanted. A guide for a lost soul.

"How are you doing?" He took her hand. It was something with that touch. She looked down at their hands. They looked like they fitted well together. Her own ring finger still had a small indentation that she might have to live with for the rest of her life. When she looked up, she saw that he studied her. In a kind way. She had trouble telling if there was anything else. What did he want? What did she want? The wine had as usual affected her.

"It's okay, or better than okay today."

She told him about the restaurant visit and the walk home. She excluded Samuel and made it sound like she only had met her best friend. Nor did she mention that she'd strolled for hours as a pastime to avoid coming home to the loneliness. The words ran smoothly in a constant stream. He understood her so well. He was such a good listener. They sat close. She felt a faint tingle in her body.

"And to think that I'm sitting here telling you all this."

"Okay, I'll be frank!"

She got a feeling that he saw right through her. All these feelings that spun in her, like ornate handwriting with no beginning and no end. A desire, a longing, but also a wish that she wasn't sitting here with Simon's friend. That it was someone else. If she only had been a few years younger, or he older. She sighed. He looked at her. She made a weak attempt to pull back her hand, but he held it firmly. She enjoyed it. Why wouldn't she?

"I wanted to talk to you, and when I saw you alone on your way home I thought I'd take the chance. I know Simon thinks it's difficult to talk to you."

Difficult to talk to me? I'm his mother!

"I don't know where to begin." He paused. "Some theories say it has to do with the upbringing. Attachment theory and other things that come into play."

Kevin was still holding her hand. His thumb caressed hers in circulating moves. A soft, almost unbearable touch. She locked her eyes on their hands. Refused to meet his gaze, afraid of falling to deeply. She was ashamed at the same time as she felt that she should be the mature one in all of this. The one who took the initiative before it even begun. But she also just wanted to cling on to him. Curl up in his arms and be taken care of. Become a little girl while

124

his strong arms held her. Let those magical soft hands caress her skin. Skin to skin. She shivered when she thought of his hands over her breasts. She felt.

"I actually don't know how to say this! It's difficult even though I think it's so simple." He laughed.

She closed her eyes and enjoyed his voice. The sound affected her, made her feel the vibrations within. A note that fitted, played with her. She wanted to sink into the feeling. She was going to enjoy it. She felt safer now and looked up to meet his eyes. His warm eyes. She would let herself drown in them. She was thirsting for love. She took her free hand and stroked his cheek. His youthful skin tickled against her fingertips. She felt her lower parts react. When was the last time she and Samuel had sex? Several years ago. She was thirsty. Starving to be touched. She wanted more.

"I don't know, sometimes words aren't needed. They just complicate things."

What she said made him look relieved. She blushed when their eyes met. Those eyelashes. Dark and thick. She leaned forward and pulled his face closer to hers. Their lips touched, and her body shivered.

Touch.

Longing.

Desire.

She pressed her breasts against him. A tear fell from his cheek and she kissed it away. The situation was getting heated and a voice told her to take what she could, another to turn it off. She didn't know how much time that had passed but realized that she'd pressed up against him and that they had ended up at the other end of the sofa.

"I'm not sure that you've understood me correctly!" The intensive moist eyes looked at her. She felt dizzy.

"Simon and I are in a relationship. We're gay."

She swallowed. Swallowed again.

Ann

Several times during the last twenty-four hours the work at the hotel had just flicked by. Eric's tense know-all-face when she'd asked for some time off. She, who had no vacation days? How would she manage? The atmosphere had been awkward, she'd disappointed him. Late last night Charlotte had turned up. They'd been up late.

The rain water from yesterday fell from the leaves, the air smelled of soil and summer. The sea was like a mirror. She placed her bare feet in the grass. Cut grass straws got stuck to her feet, she would have to cut it again before the summer party. The rain and the sun made everything grow at record speed. The cool, almost cold raindrops in the grass against her feet, made her alert. She loved these early mornings. She was alone now. Before, when the children and her husband were still asleep, this morning routine had been her elixir of life. She followed the path to the jetty. If it rained more there would be a wonderful mud to put her feet in. She lived her life to the fullest here. Enjoyed every step. A couple of mosquitos and skippers ran on the water surface. A splash came from the reeds. She stretched out on the jetty. The sunlight was already warm, and she could lie her all day and just exist. Allow herself to be tired. She needed this, she told herself, to write her notes. To find her own expression. Her previous lack of sleep had made her so tired. She slept better now. Last night she'd slept like a log. She took one day at a time. The morning swims. Making herself a tray of late breakfast. Followed her own pace. The one she'd lost in family life, a long time ago. She'd felt alone in the apartment, but here she liked her own company.

Early in life she'd told herself that she wasn't the kind of person who did nothing, then she became restless. Therefore, she would continue doing, all day long. Perform and make sure that everyone got what they needed. It had been her idea to get a summer cottage. A place to give the children those special summer holidays with sun and swimming in the archipelago. Something she'd missed as a child. She made a perfect dive. The water tightened her body. The cold found its way into every cell. She took a few strokes out before she turned back and then ran back to the house. She took off her swimsuit and put on her bathrobe. Set the breakfast table and sat down. She closed her eyes and remembered:

"Good morning, darling!"
"Good morning!"
Samuel bent down and gave her a quick kiss on her cheek. His night smell was mixed with the smells from the summer cabin.

”I must go in to the office to do some work today.”

She was surprised that he still used the word ’must’. She knew that he almost longed back to work after a couple of days in the cottage.

”I can write a shopping list. Shall we grill some fish on Saturday, maybe you can buy some from the fish market?”

”Sure, I’ll fix that. Will it be the usual gang?”

”Yes, same old, same old.”

She looked at him, he was busy trixing with a slice of bread that was stuck in the toaster. She didn’t know if he’d heard her. His lips were tense from irritation as the fork went down in the toaster, a metallic clink gave away his failure.

”Let me try.” She took the fork from him.

He sat down with a thump on the chair and she remembered that they had to tighten the screws in them. Maybe she could ask Simon to help her when he woke up. She wiped the crumbs from the table and put in two new slices in the toaster. He was already captivated by the morning paper. She had wanted to talk about the party, plan and prepare the games. She knew how difficult it would be. After all it was her persistent asking for spending the summers out here. She placed the toast on a small plate, put some butter and cheese along with a spoon of orange marmalade on it. She gave it to him. Maybe he mumbled a thank you. She sat down on the stone stairs. Soon the kids would wake up – she had plans for the day. It was her way of making the days go by, so they wouldn't become a hazy summery mess. Instead they could refer to *nail and hammer day, painting day* or *grass day.*

Simon wore his Batman swim shorts from last summer, they were too small but that didn't seem to bother him as much as so many other things. He'd pulled them up as high as possible, and in the gap between them and the t-shirt she saw a hint of pale skin. A ginger bread skin had already appeared on the rest of his body. Sun kissed tufts of hair and he had put on his cyclops. His eyes were pressed together and there was mist on the inside. She wondered if he could see anything at all. With laughter in her voice she said:

"Good morning, my lovely boy!"

"Hi, Mum." He walked up and gave her a hug where she sat on the stairs.

Her head only reached to his stomach. The warmth from his body spread over her cheek and she imagined the strong heart that crackled with joy for life in there.

"We'll have to eat breakfast first. Daddy has gone to the office and I don't want to leave Cayla alone when she's asleep."

"But Mum, I can go there myself. I can jump and swim now!" He took off the cyclops to really show her how big he was.

"You can watch me while I take a quick dip and swim to the reeds and back. And if I should drown ..." He paused and leaned towards her, "... you just jump in and save me!"

130

He leaned back again. Other eight-year olds probably got to jump in and swim on their own.

"Okay, I'll sit here, and you come up directly!" She tried to look stern. "But I think you shall take off your swim shorts so they don't get wet and you can wear them later."

"Thank you, Mum!" He gave her a big kiss. Pulled down his cyclops and pulled off his shorts. His buttocks bobbed when he ran to the jetty. Her lovely boy. She was ready with the bathrobe when he came back. He ate a big plate of porridge and was in the middle of screwing the chairs tighter when Cayla woke up. Her usual morning mood and picking in the food made Ann nervous. She sent three text messages with lists to Samuel. At lunch time she called him at the office to make sure that he'd got them. After that the rain came. The laundry got wet and there was almost no room to hang it inside. There were sheets mixed with underwear and t-shirts everywhere. Finally, sat down on the glass-enclosed veranda together with Cayla. That was one of the things she'd fallen for during the showing of the house. That and the stairs of stone. The glass, fragile and transparent, the stairs so solid and firm. Yin and yang. The contrasts. Cayla was satisfied in her lap. A single rowing boat returned after a fishing trip. They fantasized of them being princesses that were being fetched from an island. The fisherman in the boat was a prince with a big castle. Cayla ran off and put on clothes and a tiara on her head. Simon had poked out a couple of stones from it last week for his treasure, but she seemed to have forgotten that. Her eyes sparkled.

They had been asleep when Samuel got home. The laundry lay in neat piles. He had put the food properly in the cabinet and the fridge. Turned all labels to the front, that was the way he wanted it. He had been to the liquor store as well. Bought whiskey and brandy. Snaps and beer. Wine, white and red. Even if she didn't like that amount of alcohol, they actually used to have a good time at the summer party. Bibbi and Tobias. David and her mother. A few people from Stockholm that were let loose in the ar-chipelago.

Samuel had drunk a beer and fallen asleep in the sofa. She found him like that. His head sloped at the side and his feet were on the table. She felt betrayed when she saw the bottle and smelled the glass: brandy. She wished there would be less liquor when the children were present. In-stead she hoped that he would come to her bed at night. That they would wake up locked in an embrace. Because she did love him, didn't she? She looked at him. His mouth was open, and some saliva gleamed in the corner of his mouth. He snored loudly. She could never in her wildest imagination have guessed that there would be such an obvi-ous gap between them. That he chose to fall asleep in the sofa, that he chose the office instead of her and the child-ren. Above all she thought of the distance between them when she brought it up with him, wanted to talk. He just mumbled something about 'we're doing fine'. He shouldn't forget to kiss her when he came and left, or to write little notes with 'I love you'.

She put on her dressing gown and went to the jetty. The thought of putting on the wet and cold bathing suit made her shiver. She let it be. She thought of Simon's cute bottom when he'd headed to the water.

It was a bit warmer after yesterday's rain. It looked like the grass had already grown. Isn't this really the best time of the year? Summer at its best. The freedom, the lightness in her body. Here she could live at her own pace.

Charlotte and Ann

The feeling was exciting. Free like a child she dived naked into the water. Her body cleaved the water in a perfect curve. The cold water licked her body. Filled her with a positive attitude to life. Woke her up, made her ready for something new. Free and beautiful, that's how she felt. Rested and full of life. She had everything in life: a summer cottage. Children. A career as a therapist. Worked extra at a beautiful hotel. What more was possible? She swam a bit further out than usual today. Extended her strokes. There was a splash in the reeds, otherwise it was still. She turned around and floated on her back. She saw her free breasts bob in the ripples. At one time she saw the glittering hair on her vulva at the surface. Her toenails were blood-red. It was she, and nothing else, that existed right now. She enjoyed it. She continued further out. She liked to challenge herself, cross the lines. Deep down was an unknown ground. The knowledge of that excited. That deep down enticed her. An image of how one of her mother's many men had played with her in the water turned up. The game was that she stood on his shoulders and he shot up like a rocket with her, so she was thrown into the water a bit further away. It was scary every time. The man had looked surprisingly happy over the fact that she came back up. There had been a love in the game, a disappearing and a reunion. Laughter. But to her the way down towards the bottom had felt endless. Seaweed like long snakes coiled along her legs. Old leaves were turned into toads. At the bottom of the sea the imagination played freely. Created a second home. The taste of the bottom stayed on the bare child's feet.

She crawled further out, defied nature. The water got colder. Ann probably waited on the jetty. Kept a worried eye on her. The echoes of her exhortations followed her: "The undercurrents, Charlotte. Have you thought about them?" When would Ann loosen up? But who cared? She stepped up her pace, got sweaty. She breathed heavier. She got further away from Ann's restricted world. She had her own. She was free. A free woman.

She would go back into town. Make up for those long days with Ann's harping. Go out and have a glass of wine. She'd taken it easy since last time. Had avoided him. He had started something inside of her. It bothered her that he didn't want to have sex with her. He had looked at her as a friend. His gaze had not once lingered on her breasts or hips. He hadn't even seemed to notice that other men looked at her when they had returned to the bar. He'd just asked her how she felt and given her his business card. *Call me if something happens to you some night.* A quick hug. A business card. She had noticed the name John before she had let it fall down to the floor.

She swam faster.

She was out on the open sea.

Ann

She returned to the jetty. She shivered when the air got in contact with her skin. She felt her nipples harden and kind of lifted her breasts. She looked down at them. The cold made them look unusually firm from this angle. She tried to imagine how they would look from another angle and twisted her body a couple of times before she put on her dressing gown. It was so typical Charlotte to come up with the idea to swim naked. It was so childish that she let herself get carried away in these games. She was tired of sitting on the jetty waiting for her when she knew that she was afraid of the under currents. People drowned every year. Today she wouldn't pay attention to her. She needed to be alone, it was so intense with Charlotte. She needed to recognize herself. Charlotte quite often took control and steered her in directions she didn't like. She was on her way to the house when she heard a voice.

"Hello." She turned around. Tobias came paddling in a kayak.

"Hi, I didn't see you!"

"Hi, no, but I saw you!" He smiled. The kayak glided

in to the jetty. He caught the ladder with a practiced and secure hand.

How much had he seen? Had he seen her naked? She made a quick decision and pretended nothing had happened. But she felt very naked and vulnerable where she stood with her swimsuit in her hand. Her cheeks were flushed.

"How long have you been in the cottage?"

"A couple of weeks." A lump formed in her throat. Had he seen her naked? The positive attitude to life and the peace that she'd managed to reach changed into shame. She couldn't avoid noticing that Tobias flexed his muscles on his upper arms. Gigantic arms that already were chocolate brown. He probably used a solarium. He was a personal trainer on Main Street. At some point she'd walked by to see if she could get a glance of him. Wave through the gigantic windows. Someone she knew from the country. A piece of the summer a late autumn day. Samuel had never liked him. But she'd always thought that he was, well, a little sexy. She blushed.

"I have three weeks' vacation. Thought I could paddle. Like light training." He flexed his muscles again. She almost fell backwards. She'd got a splinter in her foot from the jetty and tried to focus on that instead.

"You know, you can borrow the kayak whenever you want to. It's by the jetty. Just take it. You do have a life west?"

"Yes, sure. Thank you, that's nice of you."

"See you on Saturday if not before! Looking forward to the summer party, that was like the first thing I thought about when I heard that you've separated!"

He turned around and paddled out. His back muscles worked, and he forcefully split the water with the paddle before it went under the surface. She rested her eyes on a bigger boat. In a few hours sails and spinnakers would flourish. Far away she saw the image of a swimming Charlotte, she was just a little dot. She turned to the house. Could feel her bottom wobble, her breasts were lifeless. How embarassing. Tobias of all people. He with his perfect Bibbi. She, who brought a kitchen scale with her and weighed all food. The perfect one who always said the right words and smiled the right smile. Bibbi always made Ann feel inadequate, as if she could be a little more perfect. And now she'd been standing in the nude with her unfavourable body in front of Tobias. Her cheeks flushed again. She didn't want to think about it. Better leave Charlotte out, not to tell her. She would probably only talk about how proud she should be over her body and how she could let men desire her as the beautiful woman she was. Or another cliché. Charlotte would only have asked Tobias in a jokingly manner: "Do you want to see more?" or would have said: "Damn it, Ann. Loosen up!"

Charlotte's uncomplicated hot and wild openness made her feel feeble and grey.

She made sure the bathing suit would dry in the sun, no more naked swims. She went into the cabin. The memory fragments continued where they had stopped after breakfast.

”Mum, have you seen my trunks?” held on to her like an octopus. ”Mum, do you know where they are?” His eyes beamed of eagerness and his worriless manner was contagious.

”The have to be somewhere! Have you eaten?”

Cayla picked with her sandwich. She had got some raspberry jam after some nagging. Samuel sat with deep creases in his forehead and a big glass of water. You only have yourself to blame, she thought.

”I'll get us some breakfast.”

”Yes, you have to. Daddy doesn't know what we want.” Cayla looked distrustfully at her.

”I think he knows, but he seems to be a bit tired!” The emphasis on 'tired' got a little long and drawn out. Samuel looked up sourly. She kissed Cayla on the cheek and went to Samuel. His eyes were red.

”Good morning to you to.” She kissed him on the forehead. It was sticky. She pulled her hand through his hair.

”Hey, I'm sorry”, he said and buried his head between her breasts. They stood so for a few seconds and she knew that this was precious. This was what was important in her life. The husband and the children. Some brandy every

140

now and then. He didn't drink every day. And they were on holiday.

"Stop, it tickles!" She laughed.

He buried his head deeper and took a grip of her behind. She laughed loud and bent back. His hair touched her breasts and stomach. Simon was quick in the game and Cayla said: "What about me?" before she tried to climb up in Samuel's lap. Commotion and laughter.

Cayla sounded brisk and happy when she called.

”Is it possible to moor at our jetty?”

”That depends on how big the boat is.”

”I have no idea.”

”They do know how to sail? I mean, they have charts and know how deep the boat goes?”

”Yes, relax. Of course. Wouldn’t it be fun if we showed up?”

”Yes, I guess it would.” Ann heard how vague that sounded.

”Guess?”

”You know, Daddy isn’t very fond of surprises.”

”But what about you?”

”Of course I want to meet the others. What kind of people are they?”

”They aren’t just people, they are my friends, Mum.”

”Are you seeing one of them?”

”No, I’m not!” Cayla went quiet for a few seconds.

”It’s possible to have male friends anyway!”

”Maybe so, but I care for you! I want you to be safe on the water!”

She was happy that Cayla had accepted the invitation
to the summer party, that she wanted to come after all. It
would be better if she joined the summer party instead of
sailing. Who was she to support her daughter to grow up
and become a free woman?

My growing up was characterized by men that came and went.
My father was conspicuous by his absence.
My mother chose to drink before me.

"If not, you can probably moor at Tobias' jetty."

"Yes, his perfect jetty! Great, will you check with him?"

There was a long silence. Ann had tried to imagine at
least a hundred times what her naked body had looked like
from the jetty. She had even stood in front of the mirror
and moved just like she remembered from that embarrassing situation. But she couldn't know how she had looked
in Tobias' eyes. To go over there and ask if Cayla could
moor the boat there on Saturday felt awkward. She could
ask Charlotte to do it.

"Okay, I'll ask later."

The thoughts of Tobias had come and gone. Was she
imagining that there was an attraction between them?
Maybe that was the reason Samuel never got on well with
Tobias. They wore both that kind of men that Charlotte
talked about: those who wanted to own, but in different
ways. Wanted to be in the centre and competed unaware

with each other, often about trivial material things and muscles. Women competed in another ways.

"We must become better at sharing with each other, not finding flaws. We all have a unique expression and the only responsibility is to live the way we're meant to", Mia had said.

Ann felt jittery at the prospect of the upcoming party. She and Samuel had often made a fuss before it. Argued about who should do what. She'd been whiny, he dismissal. This time she wouldn't find any flaws in him. Not ask him to do anything. But she would get unexpected support. Simon had freely volunteered to help. He and Kevin would come tomorrow. Her mother and David insisted on buying the food. The neighbour had even washed her car the other day, with the comment that "a good-looking girl needs a good-looking car" and she could accept that without feeling ashamed. That was easy to accept, simple and natural.

It's enough if you fill yourself with yourself!

To be oneself couldn't be anything but easy. Nothing that needs to be performed or fought for. Something in itself was already complete. Free to be affected by oneself. She thought about Mia, her gooseberry coloured eyes that were filled with awareness. She felt genuine. There was a naked presence, and with the permission to let others be free and affected by their expression. There was no guilt or shame.

Her thoughts were interrupted by a beep from her mobile phone. It was Charlotte.

"How are you?"

"Very well, right now!"

"You and your feelings!"

They both laughed, they knew very well that they were Samuel's words.

"So, how are you?"

"Fine, I feel up to the party. I have something for you. You're going to love it!"

"For me?"

"Yes, for you, beautiful lady. For you have caressed your breasts and explored your yoni, haven't you?"

Charlotte laughed, and Ann liked to hear it. But no, she was going to disappoint her friend. She had not acquainted herself with her yoni. But she did have fantasies of daring sexual allusions, first about Kevin and now Tobias. What was happening to her? No one had said that it would be like this over time, rather the contrary. She imagined Tobias' perfect sun-tanned body. Beautiful muscles. The obvious. His eager tongue that searched its way down her neck. Her body started to react. She saw pictures of how she lay on the jetty and spread her legs. A sexually excited Tobias who wanted her. In the next mental picture Kevin caressed her breasts. Kissed her lecherously ...

"What are you thinking about?"

"There's really no way to keep secrets from you!"

"No? I smell a rat here", Charlotte giggled.

Ann went into the narrow kitchen. There was hardly room for two. Here she had cooked a lot of convenience food over the years that had passed. She opened the kitchen cupboards. Tins and packets stood in neat rows. Samuel's system. She took out a bag and started to scoop out everything. She kept a box of macaroni and held it to her chest for a while. Simon still liked macaroni cheese. The best-before date had passed, she told herself and shoved it into the bag. Sometimes she missed the big kitchen at Winding Road. There she knew where everything was without searching for it. The loose handle on the refrigerator that used to annoy her was now a distant detail. She had nagged at Simon to get him to fix it. Why hadn't she done it herself? She'd had a vision of an equal relationship where they shared all the work and responsibilities. In her old life there had been an I-do-this and I-expect-this-in-return mentality in their relationship. She put so much of the things that reminded her of her previous life in the bag. But something pinched her irritatingly now that the tiredness wasn't as present as before. An anger was building up in her. She stamped her feet on the floor. The things on the sink unit rattled. She slammed the cupboard door. She wanted to break something. Was there nothing? She looked around, took the oak-wood cutting board with both hands and hit it hard in the sink. A metallic sound. A couple of glasses fell down in the sink. Once more. She used all her force. Bit her cheek. A vein started to throb in her forehead. She made noises. Wished she could scream. The next second her mouth opened and the sound that came out sounded inhuman.

***

Ann opened a bag of bought cinnamon buns and heated them in the oven. Made a jug of squash. She was just on her way out with a tray when she met Simon and Kevin in the door.

"Hi, Mum." He smiled at her and kissed her cheek.

"Perfect timing!" Kevin showed up behind Simon.

It was hard not to let her gaze move over Kevin. He was beautiful. These eyes. They must be among the most beautiful she'd ever seen! It was like she'd looked into them before, like visiting a familiar house after many years. He infused security. She felt a sting in her chest. She needed to talk to him about her unbounded attack in the sofa. But that also meant that she had to let go of her imagination about him. Hand him over to her son.

"Hello, Kevin!" Her voice didn't betray her, even though the throat was sore after her angry outburst. He took the tray. Their hands made contact, an electrical spark. *It wasn't the fact that he was homosexual that disturbed her, it was her*

They sat down in the arbour. The sun stood high and she realized that it would be a few different days with another rhythm. There would be people around her.

"You look really good, Mum!" Simon took a bite of his bun before he sat down.

"Thanks!"

Kevin looked at her with a look that was difficult to interpret but nodded in agreement. Had he told Simon? Or hadn't he bothered him with his mother's overstep? She bit the inside of her cheek, the bump felt tender. The tiger was calm after the outburst. The chopping board was in two pieces.

"This is a great place! Simon has told me so much about the summers he spent her, it feels like I've been here before."

"Yes, it's wonderful to be so close to nature ..." She emphasized the word 'close'.

"Doesn't it get too quiet?" Kevin wondered.

"Quiet, no. There is noise all the time. Listen!"

Both Simon and Kevin shut their eyes. Maybe that was something one did automatically to hear better. She'd started to hear vague sounds she hadn't heard for a long time. The other day she'd heard her own eyelashes against the pillow. At first, she'd got a little scared, as if she wasn't alone in the bedroom. She heard the silence. It was as if there also was a silence between every sound, a long empty sound that wasn't totally silent.

"It gets so quiet and peaceful that I just hope for a thought to pop up!"

Kevin laughed at Simon.

"I'll start the lawnmower, so you can enjoy the sound of nature."

No, don't go! Don't leave me with your boyfriend who I accosted. What had she been thinking? She'd ruthlessly forced herself upon him. Now it was too late to turn back time. There was an awkward silence. The minutes started to tick. A sinking feeling in her stomach. She should have prepared herself better for this. What did she need to say?

"It's really warm!" She fanned herself nervously with a napkin.

"You think?" He looked at her as if his thoughts had been somewhere else.

She'd moved her attention and longing from a young homosexual man to a married man. Both Kevin and Tobias were safe bets.

"I've been thinking a bit about what you said." Ann cleared her throat. She needed time to pull herself together.

"This about you and Simon being a couple. I'm okay with that, it was just me who got a bit ... well, surprised. I've been confused with all the new things happening in my life. Trying to find myself. Looking for my right tone. And that kind of came down like a bolt out of the blue. I've never

150

thought in those terms. Yet I thought that I knew Simon and that everything would continue as usual, besides the fact that Samuel and I are separated. But now I'm starting to find unexplored parts in myself. Thoughts that I haven't thought before. Maybe I'm not at all the calm housewife type that I always believed. Maybe I don't know Simon at all."

The words just poured out of her, as usual when Kevin listened. He satt calm and still as if he waited for more to come.

"Do you know Simon as a man? Or do you still see him as your little child?"

"Well, when do you know anyone?"

"Maybe when you know yourself, by knowing who you are."

Who was she, the woman who tried to get to know herself through others?

"But is this really about the other one?" Through countless hours she had listened to married couples' seemingly totally different stories.

"You have a point", she continued.

The pictures of the soft and lovely Simon as a child. The baby who turned one, and his first toddling steps. All the cosy mornings. The first day in school and his scampering on his way there. Her body was full of images and memories from the years that had passed. But never had she thought it, never had she understood. They had always been close. Had always understood each other. Didn't they know one another? How could she have missed it? Had she done something wrong?

"It's the thought of never becoming a grandmother to his child."

"Grandmother?"

"Yes, a grandmother."

Kevin laughed. "Do you really think that Simon is the children type?"

Yes, she did. Her soft, nice boy would make a great father. Didn't he like children? The letters were thrown around like to a dyslectic. The irritation grew in her. For how long had Kevin known Simon? She had known him his whole life. She knew! Simon was her child. Something bothered her. Shouldn't she know her own children best? Besides, she was so much older.

"Simon isn't your little boy any longer!"

Could she accept that all the way? Kevin and her son were a couple. If she turned the situation around, what did her mother know about her? Not much! What do I really know about the other person and his or her life?

"I'd like to see myself as the one who knows everything." Ann smiled.

"If you judge people, you have no time to love them!"
She got sucked into Kevin's eyes. Let herself be affected by

the words. The weeks in the cottage had made her soften. Something started to take shape inside her.

"That's what we do. It's easier to rise ourselves. Then we have the 'right' to judge others and label them. Gays, homos, racists or vegans, different labels!"

Kevin still looked at her.

What if compassion wasn't about the other person, rather about us? And suppose that when we judge others, we separate ourselves from our sympathy and experience the contradiction of love. She had actively tried to put all thoughts of Simon and Kevin, Tobias and even Samuel, aside in her pursuit after her own tone. Now she realized she'd only separated herself even more. She had believed that her thoughts were clouds in the sky and that her true self hid behind those clouds. But there was no sky separated from the clouds. There couldn't exist a trapped tiger without a cage. She was the one creating the cage. Who was she – she who let the surroundings be as they were, and the people she met be as they were?

I am nothing but love.

Immediately she felt a new force of energy fill her. A motion of wanting to move.

She looked again at Kevin, who regarded her.

"What's happening?"

"I feel a lot lighter and felt a sudden urge to dance."

She giggled and didn't feel as old as she'd just felt.

"You want to dance?"

He smiled. The thick eyelashes made his eyes always look warm.

Before she answered she felt how her body responded. Yes, she wanted to dance, she had never felt it more, her body had already started to move.

"Yes!"

"Then I think you should!"

She looked up at the infinite sky. The weather seemed promising. Not a cloud in the sky. An existential need. To be in the moment. She had loved to dance her whole life. She had forgotten.

She danced. The meadow rested in a summer light. The tufts of grass shimmered in the colours of the world. The place was so familiar. She'd been here before. The music filled her and without thinking she followed the moves of her body. She was free to feel them. Free to be affected. A natural drumming rhythm in her body. She shivered. There was a cold wind. She started to freeze. Small glimmering ice crystals created a surface on the ground. The frost stung her and with it came the cold. She bent down and tried to scrape the grass free. She dug and pulled the tufts to get them back. She heard the speeding train coming at her. She closed her eyes tightly.

She woke up all sweaty and didn't understand where she was before she remembered yesterday. She'd slept in the small guest room. The bed was narrow, and the room was decorated like a cabin of a boat. Kevin and Simon had the double bed. What would Samuel think when he found out? She had a bad feeling for how he would react to the fact that Simon was homosexual. She would still try not to judge him. She returned to the dream. A little different, but the discomfort was high, something ticked in her stomach. Why today of all days? On the day of the summer party. She tried to push her thoughts aside but the insight from yesterday told her that the *something* would just continue growing and get worse. She'd got Mia's private mobile number. Should she call? She glanced at the clock, half past eight. She tried to convince herself that it wasn't a defeat to call. Mia had given her the phone number freely. She'd done the same thing herself with clients who'd been self-destructive or who'd had suicidal thoughts. High fell low. She had to talk to Mia.

Mia's voice made her immediately calmer.

"At first, I thought it was pain after dancing so much. I let go of all inhibitions. I was in my body and felt motion in me. It has happened so incredible much since I moved out here, I realize that now. I thought I would wake up just as happy as when I fell asleep, but now my womb is pounding and my ovaries cramp like in menstrual pain."

"The womb can house pain and has done so since the beginning of time. But we have also been enriched with this unique organ as women: to hold life. What happens in you when I say the 'joy of living'?"

"It really hurts."

It started to pinch and pull in Ann. A ticking bomb. An image that she couldn't place showed up. A marsh somewhere, a musty smell of old moss. She didn't dare to close her eyes. She wanted the summer party to be successful. Wanted everyone to be happy and feel joy. She opened up a meeting point for everybody.

"What's happening?"

"I saw a mental picture of a swamp somewhere. I can't recall that I've been there."

"We carry a history that goes way back in time, it's in our genes. We carry the heritage in our wombs. What does your female heritage look like?"

"My female heritage? Nothing I'd like to know!" Ann laughed dryly. Her throat tightened. She coughed.

"What's happening in your body now?"

What did she think when she called Mia? That she would be healed from a distance just by talking? Did she think that she would overcome those hard parts and not have to meet the pain? At some point she must have been willing to do that since she'd called her. She'd already said yes.

"I know I can be annoying, but my inner knowledge says that if you put words to what happens inside of you, your physical pain will alleviate."

Mia was there. She knew. Ann knew.

She told her about her throat tightening, how her womb shot arrows to her throat and that she had a strong feeling that she would become free by telling her story. The one back in time. By sharing that, other women would be able to take part of it and a healing would take place at many different levels.

"There are many women who have suffered. Yes, that suffer now. I'd like to do something for them."

"There's a lot of suffering. We know each others'

stories through one other. When you try to make other women or men to fit into your world, your own suffering arises."

"So, no judging."

"A presence in yourself. Your responsibility, and it's only your responsibility to live your true expression!"

Somewhere in a shapeless haze a new seed started to sprout.

Samuel

Samuel let his gaze move over her body. New dress. It sat perfectly tight against her body. The contour of her breasts and her hips were brought out. She'd really changed since he and she ... A tug in his chest. A sensation that had become familiar. She was no longer his and that bothered him. And still it was he who had said the words less than a year ago. He who'd thrown his ring on the living room table. She walked purposefully with her bare feet in the grass. All his memories together with her, he didn't know what he should do with them. They sometimes overwhelmed him. Now it became obvious that he should have stayed at home today. This had always been her summer cottage and the summer party her innovation.

Ann had got the summer house by continually asking for it before Simon was born. When he thinks about it, it is a photographically etched memory of a very happy woman with a key in her hand and a big pregnant belly, looking out over the sea. He poked at a loose stone in the stairs. He sighed loud to make it sound like it was really too much to fix with this house. But he smiled. They would soon be a real family with a child and everything. Here, Simon would take his first toddling steps a year later. The cottage where Simon got his first tooth and two of them knocked out. Where he made her pregnant with Cayla and she throw up endlessly in the toilet. A cottage of memories to bring out under dark and gloomy winter nights. Maybe it was a financial burden, but the days were enriching and would never come back again. What was it she'd said? "In the now every minute is precious." She liked to live in the now in the minutes, feel them in her body here. It was clear that she'd blossomed since they'd separated.

He looked around. All familiar faces but yet a distance. What had Ann said about him? She didn't talk behind others' backs. She had her sence for professional secrecy even in private. But everyone here could see the change. She practically radiated. Now she blossomed. He went around and talked to everyone with a forced smile. He could always go home. The grill used to be his given place. Now David stood there with a beer and gesticulated, already tipsy.

He saw Simon.

"Hi, Dad!"

"Hi, Simon!"

They stopped at a safe distance. Simon held his hand out. He took it casually. What was the matter with him? Couldn't he hug his son just because he was gay?

"So, Kevin is here too?" He heard how stupid that sounded. He had to break his tongue-tiedness.

"Yes, he's over there!" Simon nodded towards a dark man in front of Ann. She looked at Kevin with that little special smile he'd only seen her smile when she was with people she liked. Didn't that Kevin guy stand a little too close to Ann to be homosexual? Another tug in his chest and a sting of familiar jealousy came over him. He couldn't get rid of the feeling that he missed her. That soft smile. He missed that as much as all the other daily things. How she still half asleep breastfed in the middle of the night. The shuffling sound of her slippers when she patted away to make morning coffee and her hair was still flat on the back of her head. Everything that had bothered him seemed to get his hold on him in an endless haze. She and he were now only a parenthesis in life. He felt half without her.

Simon had left him, and he steered towards David who unaffected smiled big with his furrowed face. They had always had a special connection. Even if alcohol was the glue. They had developed a unique talent to vanish together when Ann and her mother argued. He missed what had been!

David handed him a beer.

"You look like you need a couple of these."

"Oh, it's that obvious?"

"Yes, and I know the feeling."

He had actually planned to drive back home. He felt the cold beer in his hand and considered it. If he drank, he wouldn't be able to flee back home. He had even told his flirt that he'd show up later. A small relief for the ache in his chest.

"Cheers!" David chuckled.

"Yes, cheers to the summer party!" With mixed feelings Samuel drank the beer in one go. David gave him another in one hand and put the grill fork in the other.

Samuel stared in Ann's direction. She was talking to Tobias. The narcissistic neighbour. He was such a bastard towards women. Without further consideration he went up to them. He instinctively put his arm around Ann's waist and kissed her cheek. He became calm when he felt her scent. He felt so at home here. He noticed that she tried to pull away, but he took a more resolute grip around her waist. He held the grill fork in the other hand. If he'd been the man that before had made her look pale, it was time he changed that! He was going to have her!

The doors were open, the music boomed even though Ann had turned down the volume several times. When she came in, she heard laughter and loud voices. Cayla was in a great mood and her male friends seemed really nice. The whole house was turned upside-down. There was verve and spirit when Cayla was in this mood. Ann gave her daughter a long hug. She missed not seeing her every day. Cayla smelled of perfume. A fresh scent. She was becoming a woman now, young and unexperienced. Maybe one of her friends would take her virginity. Or already had done it. She wished that they could get some time alone together to talk.

"Mum, can I do your make-up, please?"

"Yes, sure!" She moved a chair into the bathroom and sat down. The new surprise dress from Charlotte was still on its hanger. Small cerise and blue butterflies sailed all over the natural-coloured background. It fitted perfectly. She had tried it on twice already. The fabric emphasized her body in a feminine way. Not to seductive, yet provocative. So typical Charlotte. Ann looked in the mirror. The sun-bleached hair fell loose over her shoulders. Sometimes she felt bleak but today she really radiated. Her eyes sparkled. Cayla had done a good job with her make-up. The difference was visible. She straightened. Felt nice. Felt like dancing again.

”Cayla, what an amazing change!”

”Mum, it's you who are beautiful! On the inside, don't forget that!”

It could have been her own words. Created before she left her daughter at preschool one early morning while Cayla held a tight grip around her neck.

Cayla was already out with the others and she heard her giggle. Which one of the boys was hers?

Ann pulled the dress over her head. She had bought a new bra and briefs. Just because. Allowing herself something new. She'd put Samuel's things in a bag, she was going to ask him to take them with him later. Yes, home. This was her home now. Winding Road had faded. The apartment felt far away.

The temperate summer evening wellcomed her when she came out from the house. Her arms were bare. The dress billowed around her legs. Her hips moved. She walked barefoot in the grass. The party mood had started and was perfect. People were laughing, and they enjoyed being together. She liked it when people were gathered.

”Do you have something to drink?” It was Tobias. ”I'll get you something, what do you want?” Intensive gaze.

Just get something, or rather, leave me alone. It started to buzz and roar in her ears. The surroundings disappeared. She was no longer

"A glass of rosé, please!"

He soon came back.

"Cheers to you, you look wonderful tonight!"

"Thank you!"

Her lips got tighter in what could look like a sugary smile. His white t-shirt seemed to blind her, and the smell of fabric softener tickled her nose. He wore a pair of black shorts with a wide belt. Simple, nice. Advertisingly fresh.

Samuel, who she'd seen knock back a beer with David by the grill suddenly showed up and placed his arm around her waist. A mark. He also kissed her cheek. She started to get annoyed. What was he thinking?

What if they swapped places, so it was Tobias who stood with his arm around her waist?

She managed to get away from Samuel's arm and made sure everyone got what they wanted. The dinner passed, she could feel Tobias' intensive eyes from the other side of the table. She wasn't surprised when she, out the corner of her eye, saw him follow her to the kitchen. Tobias was quick to put on the music. She'd always been fascinated over the fact that men could start any electrical equipment with their remotes so easily.

"You've got great music", he called from the living room.

She bit her cheek. Cayla's taste in music. A quick glance in the window reflection, she was alright. What was she doing? Had she fallen in love with Tobias? It all felt absurd. She'd been married to Samuel. This was still their summer cottage. Tobias had the perfect Bibbi.

Ann small talked nervously. She hardly knew what she was doing. There was an electrical tension in her body. A tingling she'd been missing, yet it terrified her. The narrow kitchen made it difficult to avoid that their bodies touched.

She excused herself to go to the toilet. She needed to cool down. He didn't make it easy for her, she had to squeeze passed him where he stood in the doorway. The door had been taken down, but the hinges were still there, she noticed that he held his hand on the top hinge. There was not much room for her to pass. For a second, he held her there in the doorway. Time stood still – she must have looked horror-struck. He twisted a strand of her hair around his finger.

"Your hair looks nice, too."

"Thank you." She slipped away. Locked the door to the toilet and sunk down on the toilet seat with a sigh. Her fingers shivered. She was excited. The feelings tugged at her. She must find her common sense. A logical explanation to why she felt the way she did. The rosé wine soared through her veins.

A quiet knock on the door. Her breathing got stuck in

her throat. A knock, as muffled as if someone didn't want it to be heard. Maybe it was her imagination? The lump in her throat grew. She couldn't let Tobias in. That just wasn't an option! This was her and Samuel's toilet. They hadn't divided everything yet. She needed this sanctuary now. How limitless could he be? She bit the inside of her cheek and heard Charlotte's voice.

"It's me."

What a relief, she breathed out with a sigh. She could tell Charlotte about Tobias.

"Are you alright? What are you doing in here?"

"I needed to breathe."

"I'm going for a swim."

Ann's eyes widened. "Swim? No, not me!" She sunk down to the seat again. Her hands were a bit shaky and she locked them in her lap.

"I didn't mean that you should do it." Charlotte smiled, a smile Ann hadn't seen for a long while. The teenage smile. The revolt.

"That's the reason I came here. You must help me!"

Ann's already big eyes got bigger. Ann saw that she'd had a little too much wine. She always got excited and probably shouldn't drink since her mother almost had drunk herself to death before she took her own life.

"It's Tobias", Charlotte said and got an indefinable look Ann found hard to interpret. So, she had noticed it? How she, Samuel's ex-wife, was attracted to Tobias' electrically sparkling muscles. Anne felt the lump in her throat and that she was getting a headache. What was she doing?"

"Do you know, Tobias wants us to go swimming, him and I. Just the two of us!" Charlotte looked excited. "Well, maybe you've seen the way he looks at me! It's like he locks me with his gaze. And I thought ..."

Everything went black before her eyes. The ground shook under her. Splash. Ice cold water. Ann couldn't really hear. The words fell away. A mouth that moved and popped the bubble. She only had one choice: to once again get back in the loyal armour. She was the therapist, mother of two who hosted the annual ongoing summer party. All the usual things fell in place. Charlotte and Tobias. They were going to start something. She was nothing more than a bystander. She'd imagined it all. The intense look. His helpfulness in the kitchen had been for Charlotte, not her.

"What about Bibbi?" She whispered the words. Raised her eyebrows in a reassuring manner and bit her cheek. The lump on the inside was now big as a marble. Her own wishes tried to get out of her like dandelions in the asphalt. *But what about me?* As if someone had held a delicious chocolate cake with frosting in front of her but pulled it away before she'd had a chance to taste it.

Charlotte and Tobias.

"Yes, that's the thing. Could you talk to Bibbi for a while and keep her busy? Please!" Charlotte held her hands in front of her like she was praying.

"Please?"

"Did Tobias tell you to ask?"

"No, it's my idea. You and I are best friends."

Samuel and Ann

All Ann could do was to find Bibbi. The incipient headache got worse with every step. She felt sick and wanted
to be alone again, but nobody else seemed to notice anything. The party mood and the music went on, but inside
of her she had conflicting feelings. The tiger roared. All
the years she and Charlotte had known each other she'd
always been jealous of the freedom and openness Charlotte
represented. So close to laughter. They were different. But
now she felt dislike. Cheated of her own fantasies. Alone
with a headache.

Samuel was at his best and looked as if he was solv-
ing all the problems in the world over a bottle of brandy
together with David. Ann guessed they would both have a
tough day tomorrow. Samuel got sight of her and hurried
up to her.

"We need to talk!" He took her arm a little too hard.

"Not today. Not now, Samuel." She sounded more irritated than she intended.

"Yes, now!" He led her behind the hedge of lilacs.
There was a lounge suite of hand carved birchwood she'd

got on her fortieth birthday. A beautiful craftsmanship. Her hand stroked the wood before she sat down. The light dress would get damp from the dew. Maybe get stained.

"You're avoiding me!" He sat down heavily, clearly drunk.

"So?" The last thing she wanted to do was to have a discussion with a woozy ex. Their usual pattern. How many times had he ignored to listen to her? How often had she not wanted to express her feelings? How could he at all think that she would be here for him now?

"Who are you seeing?" He stared at her. The skin around his eyes looked tired. Upset, he pulled his hand through his hair, as to see if it was still there.

There was something recognizable in the whole situation. Her childhood. The ill-timed comments from the men.

The headache pounded between her temples. To let him talk and just listen wasn't in her interest. He'd turned out to be unreasonable regarding their finances. Had not been willing to talk about feelings for a long time. She wasn't going to coddle him anymore or compromise the way he was used to. She was going to try a new approach. Maybe she couldn't turn the ship all the way around today, but at least get a firm grip of the rudder. The road would show her the way to what she wanted.

Who was she who stayed in her tone?

"Who are you seeing? Who? Is it someone I know? At the hotel, right?"

"As if that matters, Samuel." The lump in her cheek started to bleed.

"So, you *are* seeing someone?" He leaned forward, his eyes shining black. His blunt manner made her instinctively flinch.

Her feelings were conflicted. Tobias. Simon and Kevin. Cayla's young body that danced with her different male friends. Bibbi who waited. She had promised Charlotte. *"They are like young boys, don't ever forget that."* Somewhere in the haze she could hear her mother's voice. She wanted to scream at Samuel, let the tiger free, let it tear him to pieces. The headache boomed.

Take the rudder, Ann.

It would have been so comfortable if she hadn't met Mia. But she knew better. She had a responsibility, and that responsibility was to follow her inner expression.

"No, Samuel, I'm not seeing anyone. I'm trying to sort out my life. Catch up with myself."

He scrutinized her to see if she was telling the truth. He was also aware of the stroke of jealousy that could wake up at any time. They had talked about it for hours in therapy.

She sat calmly. Everything was still. There were many questions. The treasure map lay hidden. She didn't need to

172

know everything right now. All she needed to do was to hold the rudder so the boat didn't capsize. He had *no* right to her any longer. She wouldn't push him away. Wouldn't let him in. Hold the rudder, Ann. Hold your own.

It has nothing to do with the other one!

Estrid

Estrid was woken up by something warm streaming down her legs. Her breasts ached. When her eyes got used to the darkness, she saw her sister's outlines appear by the fire. What was it she held? Her thoughts spun. She felt feverish, warm and cold at the same time. There was a worrying burning sensation in her lower parts. At once she remembered: Sigrid's contorted face. A scream. Sharp pain that had welled over her. The women's anxiety. The child held at a distance. Then a total darkness.

"Eira?" Her voice was choked and powerless.

"She's here. Asleep. Everything's fine with her."

Her sister placed the bundle next to Estrid. She had fever, but the child was alive.

"You've lost a lot of blood. The placenta didn't come out intact. It looks like you can't stop bleeding. How do you feel?"

Her sister kneeled before her. Her worry reflected in the dark. The question hung silently in the air. The only thing she heard was the breathing from the baby and the crackle from the fire.

Eira cautiously took the breast. A shiver went through Estrid's body when the breast milk begun to flow. The baby was unharmed. Her sister had taken care of them both. She wanted to ask what they'd done with the placenta but didn't dare. She didn't want to be reminded of more blood.

The days passed by in a haze. Outside life went on. She heard the animals. The children that quietly came in to her with expectant glances. The women who helped her. Estrid enjoyed being alone with Eira. The light around the baby shone like gold in the gloomy house. When their eyes met, she was filled with affection. She saw the beauty of life through her own eyes while the little one found the breast. She had never felt anything like it before. She was complete. She closed her eyes pleasurably when the little mite noisily sucked her milk. As if she remembered an old dream, she saw herself dance in a glade with her daughter in her arms. Wonderful tones of a limitless state. She had borne a child of the gods. The conviction that had grown during the pregnancy. The sign of nature. This was a special girl.

The days changed shape, the autumn gave fruits late in November and the snow came as a quiet blanket. The men had not returned as expected. Estrid didn't think a lot about it and the children stopped asking. She slowly healed. They'd run out of healing herbs a long time ago. She looked forward to pick horsetail and lomme. She helped out with what she could but quickly got feeble and tired. Eira laughed happily, ate, thrived and grew. Her sister worked for two. Estrid couldn't stop looking at the little one. So whole and clean. She preferred to be alone with her. The other women held a distance to them both as if they were contagious. She understood them, first Sigrid's deformed child and now her. Broken placenta, the nutriment that was sucked out of the tree of life. And the men who had not returned to the tribe, to the pack. Not a good omen.

Sigrid often moved around outside the house. Sometimes she came in and stared at Eira.

"There's something wrong with that girl", she said one day to her sister.

"The sorrow's got hold of her." Her sister answered without looking up. She continued to weave.

"She brings bad luck!"

"We must stay together, it looks like it'll be a harsh winter." Her sister's face was tight and tense. The eyes never left her weaving. Estrid knew what she was thinking of: how they would manage if the men didn't come back. The heavy feeling of faith covered the camp. The cold seeped deeper into them. Estrid and Eira were welded together to a beautiful sword. Iron bars that were heated until they were transformed to steal. That thereafter were twined together with similar bars to a solid and pliant mix of steel and iron. The one couldn't live without the other. She had thought about it. Eira and she, two became one. Nothing could separate them or take what she and Eira had together.

Sigrid disturbed her at night. She could hear her steps around the camp. Her stillborn son haunted her in her dreams. She woke up soaked in sweat. One night she thought she saw Sigrid leave the house. She'd called for her, but no one had answered, only Eira had woken up and looked at her with her big eyes. As if she understood. The winter became harsh. They had to move in together to keep warm, the

176

food was rationed. They were pale and weak from malnutrition. More death awaited, and no one talked about the men's absence. The future was uncertain.

Winter became spring. The sun was longed for. The women rarely talked about the men. They did what they were supposed to do, and the year went by. The children had stopped asking. The little one's blond curls tickled Estrid in her face when she looked up at the faint April sun. She was filled with a sense of satisfaction. It was a peculiar little girl she'd given birth to. An extra chosen. She had a special bond to Eira.

Suddenly she needed to pee and pulled up her skirt. It was still cold outside and when the cool air reached her backside she whimpered. There was a sharp burning sensation that never seemed to go away. The herbs didn't help anymore. She adjusted the piece of felted wool she used as a protection between her legs. The little girl turned to her and caressed her cheek. Eira had a healing power, she wasn't like the others. Her glowing eyes that pierced through you, that saw, that knew. Everybody noticed it. The siblings' distancing. The women's fumbling insecurity. Estrid had early understood that she had to protect her daughter.

Inside of Estrid a horrible image had been born, but she didn't dare to talk about it. Not even with her sister. Sigrid would try to take Eira from her. She knew it, the birds whispered it in her ears.

Bibbi

Bibbi looked lost and confused when Ann flopped down on an empty chair. As always, Bibbi looked young and fresh. She had a white linen dress. The manicured hands clutched tight around a bottle of mineral water that she sipped from.

Ann wanted more rosé and her eyes searched for a bottle on the table. Her headache and the tension had become worse after she left Samuel. She couldn't let go of his black eyes.

”Hello, Ann. I must say that you look really nice tonight!”

”Oh, thank you!”

She felt ungainly next to Bibbi, not at all beautiful anymore and wanted the party to be over. A closed chapter in her life. What had she been thinking when she invited everyone to the party?

”It's so great that there was a party even this year. It's always so nice to come here.”

”Do you think so?” Her own question surprised Ann.

”Yes, why wouldn't I?” Bibbi looked offended and looked into the bottle as if she would find something there.

"Well, I just realized that I don't know what you like."

Like the fact that your husband is now swimming with my best friend!

Truth to be told, her image of Bibbi was that she was the one who wandered about restlessly at the party. An aquaintance that she'd felt obliged to make small talk to every year. The only thing she knew was that Bibbi and Tobias met at a party nearly five years ago. One time, she had turned up for a cup of coffee, but they hardly knew each other. She'd always found it difficult to listen intensely to Bibbi, she felt bored and realized that she preferred to avoid her.

"... yes, it's been a few years now, as you know." She pulled her hand through her hair and smiled a little at the memory and continued:

"He came home with me." She'd said no, thought it went to fast, but he had coaxed her and soon after they were a couple.

"Oh." Ann nodded. "What happened then?" She'd missed what Bibbi was talking about.

"Tobias couldn't understand that I liked it better in the city than in the country. Sure, the place he's inherited here is really nice, but I longed to go back to my apartment in the centre of Stockholm."

"Okay, if I understand you right, Tobias wanted to live

here?" Ann pointed at the big yellow house.

"I couldn't understand that Tobias was so keen on it. If we rented it out it wouldn't cost us anything extra. Besides, I had my work at the bank." Bibbi looked down at her mineral water again. "We'd talked about it the first three months and I couldn't understand why he was so upset. He never gave in."

"What did you do? Let go of your apartment?"

"Tobias has a tendency to easily feel rejected and angry, you see."

"Don't you want it to work out between us?" His voice was hard and sharp.

"Yes, and you know that I want that." Bibbi's eyes tried desperately to find Tobias', who in protest had moved to the other end of the sofa.

"Yes? That doesn't sound very inviting, say yes loud and clear!"

"Yes, I say yes. I've said it several times." She felt the desperation in her voice but was careful not to raise it.

"I've chosen you! I don't understand why you need to have an apartment. Don't you trust me?"

"Of course I do."

"I don't get it. Why?"

"But I've told you many times that I want to keep it so it's there if something happens between us."

"So, you're planning for something to happen?"

"No, I don't mean it that way."

"What do you mean?"

"That if I sublet my apartment it doesn't cost anything. I don't understand why that should affect us now."

"You're changing directions all the time. Have you already met someone else?"

"Of course I haven't, darling." She moved a little closer. The distance between them made her feel insecure. "Of course it's the two of us."

"Right then, give up your apartment! If not, you don't want it to work out. You do want me to trust you?"

Bibbi closed her eyes. She didn't get anywhere. If she couldn't end this now it would be like so many times the last few months. She was weighed down. A tear was welling up. She really loved him. He was everything to her. He had found the key into her heart. She'd never before felt this way. So natural. The perfect couple. Soul mates. She had promised herself to never become dependent on a man. She would stand on her own two feet. Strong and stable.

"If you say no, it's because you don't trust me and can leave me and go back."

"Okay, I'll let go of the lease."

Tobias moved closer to her. She moved closer. They met in the middle of the sofa.

"I knew you would be sensible."

He caressed her back. She felt so safe in his arms. Big strong arms that held her.

He would save her from everything.

"And you will show me that the lease is terminated?"

I am everything to him.

"Yes, of course!"

He softly caressed her hair. He had everything. The gift
of speach. Lots of feelings and was good looking. She lost it
every time she looked at him. The only thing that had disturbed their harmony was her apartment. She really didn't
need to keep it. Her love to him meant a lot more than the
apartment. He wanted to be sure that she stayed with him
forever. He had said that he only chose the best. She, the
best. They were best for each other.

He continued stroking her hair.

"It's so different with you, Bibbi. I have never felt like
this. You are the best thing that's happened to me! You
know I only pick the best!"

"What happened then?" Ann's curiosity had woken up.
Bibbi sat with tears in her eyes, obviously affected by the
feelings that had controlled her life. Ann put her hand on
her arm.

"He ..." She blew her nose loudly. "He kind of made
me want to have sex."

He cupped her breast with his hand under the sweater

and undid her bra with the other hand. Then he tore off her clothes. The haste astounded her. She really must mean a lot to him. So direct, yet it turned her on. She hadn't gone to bed with anybody without making sure there was a foreplay and an after play. But she had misinterpreted herself. She liked this new way of making love. Bang on. Sporty. Like a sprint, an exotic exercise. He made her feel sexy and hot.

Bibbi started to work part time. She accompanied him to the gym. They worked out and made love. The spent every second together. Inseparable. The few times they had to be apart was an ordeal. It was like separating the egg white from the yolk in a whipped eggnog.

"Wow, what a story. Thanks for sharing it!"

Ann was touched. This thing with sharing one's female history with someone, to receive and listen to the words without judging. Just like Mia had done. The listening. The presence reminded her of something complete without separation. We belong together, us women. Ann sat quiet for a while, still with a hand on Bibbi's arm while the noise around her returned. She'd been absorbed and almost forgot where she was. She felt gratitude for having had the chance to take part of somebody else's thoughts and feelings, so close. Bibbi looked more relaxed now. She was a beautiful woman. What had made her choose a man like Tobias? Or that she herself had felt the way she'd done for him?

”I think that we women need to be better at staying firm in what we believe in! All you need to do is to fill yourself with the whole of you!” Ann got up.

”Come, beautiful woman!” She held her hand at Bibbi who dried her eyes with the napkin. Bibbi hesitated.

”What are we going to do?”

”We shall dance, come!”

The music found its way to the lawn and hand in hand they let their feet caress the tufts of grass.

Charlotte

He made her thoughts wander. Made her loose the conception. The feeling of wanting was taking over everything. The touch made her legs go numb. She moistened between her legs and felt a faint scent from her willing body. Her hips started moving. She pressed her lower parts against him. The bulge under the shorts woke her horniness. She wanted him now! She unbuttoned his shorts and caressed him over his stomach. He moaned softly. His hand had found her breast. Gently he released her from the bra. He let his fingertips circle around her nipple. She heard herself whimper. Her hand searched further down. The swollen shaft throbbed in her hand. Perfect size. His hand on her breast and their tongues that searched each other. Their moves got more intense. He took an awaiting step and studied her, still with his hand on her breast. It pulsated. A warming intensity. It was something in the way he looked at her that made her horny. Suddenly, she felt shy. What if he didn't feel as she did. She wasn't seventeen any longer. Her body had flaws and countless stretchmarks. But in the dusk, she could let go, thoughts about her imperfect body wouldn't stop her now. Now that he finally was with her. She'd been longing and dreaming.

"I must taste you!" His head moved down between her legs. She tried to cover herself with her hand, but his eager tongue found its way between the fingers. The tip of his tongue tickled her clitoris, he used his other hand to reach better. His tongue played. Everywhere. She felt exposed and surrendered to just feel. She felt pleasure like never before. She gave him permission by pressing against the searching tongue.

She was beautiful.

She was good.

She loved it.

She raised her arms over her head and when she was close to climax he let the stubble scratch lightly on her belly with his chin. She looked at him. Her body wanted. He knew it and how to make her reach her climax. The swollen male organ. She couldn't take her eyes off it. She yearned, she wanted it inside of her. Feel it work. A drop of semen shone on his glans. All of a sudden, she felt thirsty. She met his eyes. He smiled. He knew what she was thinking. With his eyes locked in hers he let his tongue touch her clitoris again. She'd had time to cool down a little and he let his warm tip taste her. His chin pressed against her opening and he looked into her eyes. Again, he stimulated her in a way she never could have imagined in her wildest fantasies. She heard herself moan far away, maybe she screamed.

186

When the orgasm came her body was shaking. The vibrations spread in her whole body. Every cell inside of her was
smiling.

Torvald

Torvald saw Estrid from a distance. He'd been gone far too long, and it wasn't until he was on his way home that he thought about his wife. Had she given him another son? The thoughts of Sigrid had also been there, her slender body against his. Sigrid was beautiful and satisfied, not so harsh and resolute as Estrid. Now he saw how beautiful Estrid was in the sunshine. Her hairslide glimmered in the sun. The linen fabric was new and around her legs a little one toddled about. He was longing to take her warm and soft body into his arms.

"Estrid!" The sound echoed in the nature and came back to him.

She put the basket down. Her face smiled and Torvald walked up in a rapid pace. He lifted her with strong arms before he hugged her. He could hear her heart beat. He took in her smell from her neck. It was sweet and smelled of smoke.

Torvald studied Estrid when she combed their daughter's hair. Eira had her mother's beauty. They seemed to have an odd relation to each other, as if the others couldn't reach them. To his annoyance, Eira always woke up when he searched for his wife's warmth. Very quick a sting of jealousy had risen, and now there was even hatred in his eyes.

Sigrid had often showed up and laughed with him. He noticed that Estrid didn't like Sigrid.

It was just before the snow fell and the camp was busy. The food and the mead spoke of good hunting. Torvald had put his daughter in his lap and kissed her good night. When everything was quiet, Torvald went to see Sigrid.

Meanwhile, Estrid took farewell of her sister. Eira slept in her arms. No one could ever take away their love from her. They were inseparable. That was the comfort she took with her when she stepped out in the pitch-black night. Of the new that awaited her she knew nothing, just that she had to go. A woman's travel in time.

Ann

It seemed to get greener and greener every day. She reached
for a blade of grass and put it in her mouth. It would soon
change, and Ann tried to suck in as much as possible of
the summer. It was the freedom the summer cottage offered. But what would it be like if she lived here the whole
year? Would it be better to just remember everything that
had been and sell the place? The thought of a for sale-sign
gave a pricking sensation in her midriff. This afternoon she
was going to see Mia, she had mixed feelings. The summer
party was still like dirty dishes in a washing-up bowl. She'd
have to stand up for herself. That was big to her. She knew
that much, she needed to become a free and independent
woman. But not at other women's expense.

Mias voice made her calm. There was something rebellious over her presence. It was that feeling of her being
there, listening beyond the words. She had fun at her place
today. Laughed at her own thoughts. Life felt hopeful there.

"What do you think about taking a look at your values
of men, Ann?"

Boom, it was like a slap in her face!

”What do you mean with values? Men?”

”Your conceptions of men. Come on!”

The inner laughter threatened to go away, the echo subsided. It had started so well. She’d felt ready to come out from her own bubble today. She tried desperately to push away her thoughts.

Would her thoughts of men affect her? The world? It was a universal truth that it was men who committed the most crimes. That it was common with women battering. Every third woman had been subject to violence in a close relationship. All of a sudden, she was tired.

She went to the window. The crown of a tree blocked out most of the view, but beyond it she saw cars and a few people that moved. Men and women that stressed towards personal goals. Women and men separated from each other. People who bustled on in life on the outside. On an escape from themselves. Separated from knowing life through life.

What would happen if I started to feel again? What would happen if I allowed myself to live as complete as I once was?

So, who am I: the woman that is no longer ruled by old notions on how men work? Who am I as a complete woman? I don’t have to try to satisfy men, not change them, not fight. Not change me or them.

”Today I want to try the massage bench. ”I want you to massage my stomach.”

"Your stomach", Mia repeated calmly. But Ann thought she saw a glimpse of something in her eyes. As usual, Mia seemed to understand things about her before she did it herself.

Mia had invited to trust, her hand rested on Ann's stomach. A presence that made Ann relax more and more. She sank deeper into herself. She determined the pace. She decided over her body.

"I want you to say the word 'men' and tell me what comes to mind."

"It was cold outside."

She was so cold that she shivered. She was also lacking something. Then she heard the train coming. With that horrifying, deafening sound. Her body tensed. The womb clenched to a lump. Mia talked soothing to her, asked her to welcome all feelings and every thought. Ann was on her way of losing herself in a deeper fear. She looked up. Mia looked peacefully at her. She was still there. Her own fear didn't seem to disturb her.

Mia moved her hand in a circle and massaged the area over her womb. She took a few drops of sweet-scented oil. Ann's body was accommodating. The cramps slowly gave in.

"Be curious, explore, meet the word 'men'. What do you see?"

"I see a ball of some kind, tangled like a ball of yarn that isn't supposed to be there. It's on one of my ovaries."

It was as if Mia had understood her. "There is no such thing as logic here. You can start untangling that ball of yarn."

Quiet again for a while. Her fear subsides when she starts to untangle it. Her hand is still cramping but Mia's hand works rhythmically and methodically.

"What's happening?"

"It hurts, I want to scream but it's not possible. I lay still, they say that I want to. Because I'm not screaming."

"How many are they?"

"Six, seven."

"Who's the seventh? Again, here's no logic. It's the memory of your cells that shows you the way."

She has confidence in Mia's calm manner.

"It's him, Chris."

"Who's Chris?"

"The guy from the New Year's party."

"What's he doing?"

"I mustn't tell!"

"What happens if you do?"

"I will die!"

"Truthfully, what is it that is not allowed to be spoken aloud?"

"He's selling me!"

The pain increases. The tangled ball explodes, erupts in a cascade of lava. It's burning inside of her, a pain like no other pain. She thinks that she's going to have a baby, that a lump of five kilos will come out even though she's not open. Someone has stitched her up. She wants to tear away Mia's hands as if they are the Devil. She screams. She hits the bench. Her body is tossed from side to side. Finally, she moans and then starts sobbing. She wishes that Mia could hold her like a child, but there is no child to hold. There is a woman. Mia's hand moves on over her stomach.

That boy had offended her with his words. The same boy that later said that he would kill her if she uttered a word about what had happened. He became the man who repeatedly changed the subject to blame the woman. She saw. She'd become indifferent over the years. Locked her pain inside a tangled ball, a defence mechanism.

If I'm not a woman I cannot get hurt!

My mother wasn't there for me, just like so many other women in the past have not been aware and present women. I tried to compensate that by creating my own version of a fairy tale to give my children what I never had. My children would have sober, responsible parents who made them feel safe. No men that came and went. She could make sacrifices. The sweet forgetfulness of denial, she was acquainted with it. Sacrificing, to give up your own life for another, for peace in the family. Was that an act of love? To disregard one's own needs for another? Or satisfy other's needs before her own? Why couldn't both persons' needs

194

be satisfied in a meeting? Tones that met without demands.

For a long time, she thought she needed to change. That she was wrong. Samuel had said that women were complicated. But those were his words, not hers. This wasn't about somebody else. She needed to stay in what she was destined to be. If women allowed themselves to be true to themselves. If she followed her inner compass. Men could be men. It was there the complication lay.

So, who was she? She was outside her comfort zone now. Explored who she was beneath all musts and all the fixing. It felt big, as if she was on her way of finding something greater, something that all women of the world had the right to forcefully enter. It wasn't about fighting for women's rights and castrating men. It was about living one's natural inner being to the fullest. Follow one's inner needs and live in harmony with the person one was destined to be. In the history of earth, the woman has had to leave room for the man. Put her intuition aside and create a world that would satisfy him. Now these women danced freely at the men's sides, they invited to dance.

"I've felt alone in the twosomeness. Outside. All my life I've had a wish to meet *Him*. He, the only one, the right one, and experience happiness, a togetherness. A knowledge and what I thought was divine love. All of that just disappeared, all wishes and hopes were taken away from me. Like a rug pulled away from under my feet and I fell. But now it feels as if my body and I belong together, as if we are the same and it's a body of one. A case to harbour something divine. I will no longer search for who I am with my words. I will feel in an existence."

"What if he isn't a he, but a she?" Mia sounded confident and continued: "Like two parts of an apple that shall heal to a complete apple."

She showed with her hands. Two halves that were put together to something whole.

Charlotte

Should it be like this to become fifty? She felt weaker, the age seemed to make her unnoticeable, as if a transparent layer dissolved her whole existence. Her skin had slowly lost its elasticity, it looked as if it was paper-thin. She brushed her shoulder long hair with a few strokes and made a braid with trained hands, stroke a couple of grey hairs behind her ear. She was running out of mascara, the same unnoticed change as life went on. She pulled on a pair of training trousers and a grey tank top. The sports jacket of the same brand matched. Since the summer party she had gone from being relatively fit to muscles and weight that had disappeared unnoticed. Her sweatpants sat loosely. She made sure everything was in her bag and threw it over her shoulder. The air was fresh outside, one of the charms with early mornings. If it hadn't been for Ann, she would have stayed in bed a couple of hours more. But Ann needed her now. Her support, someone to lean on. Spiritual sisters had to be there for one another. Ann had needed her during all these years of denial. Her duty had been to bring out the woman in Ann, who had fallen under shame and guilt. The collective guilt of the Universe. She'd many times doubted if Ann would manage. Ann's connection to Samuel was, according to Charlotte, only pathetic loyalties. Which married man could be faithful? It was all hypocrisy, men went after everything that moved. Ann tried not to judge the men and continued to play hide-and-seek behind her role as a therapist. When life was fragile and hung on a string, Charlotte had always been there. All the way she had been there for Ann. But where was Ann when she needed her? A kind of a slow awakening, a very painful one! Ann turned her back to her. Circumstances were abruptly thrown into her face. Was that her thank you after all these years?

It was Friday and she walked home with heavy steps. It was pay day and that meant her mum was having a party, everybody would be drunk. The child benefit and other money from social security payed the rent. She wished she was someone else. She hadn't drunk anything since New Year's Eve, hardly smoked either. Refused to become like her mother. The sheer thought of herself living together with a greasy boozer gave her the creeps. She would never get stuck in drinking. Yes, David was nice, but she hated him just as much as she hated her mother. Every now and then the thoughts of that guy from New Year's Eve popped up. Small fragments had flicked by the last six months. A few vague words and how she'd composed herself to get from the suburb in the morning. How she had, still drunk, stumbled out from his hall. Staggered out into the cold on her high heels. Her vagina ached. It was burning and felt dry. That guy was just like all of her mother's numerous men!

Charlotte stood stomping for a long while outside the yoga class. Wasn't Ann going to show up? After all these years that she'd been there for her.

Ann

Early morning had always been her favourite time. She slept better now, and changes became visible in her life. The glitter in her eyes met her in the mirror. Her lips appeared more marked. She straightened, scrutinized the woman in the mirror. She accepted what she saw. She had cast off her role as the victim. Even though Charlotte had insisted on the two of them taking the yoga class together, she didn't want to go. She'd started to question whether they really were as good friends as she'd thought. There was something strange about Charlotte, her rebellious and seductive hints started to annoy her. Why couldn't they talk about Tobias? Charlotte acted indiscreetly and without boundaries since the summer party. Tried to play the role of the angel that came to the rescue even when Ann hadn't asked for it. Like when she'd told her about the last session with Mia. She had wanted to tell her about the New Year's Eve.

It's cold outside and she doesn't know what has happened. Just that something in her have changed. Separated.

Charlotte had looked at her with envy. Her facial muscles had twitched with anger, something she'd never noticed before. Her eyes had turned black. The same despise her mother showed to diminish men. Castrate them, as Mia called it.

They are like little boys, don't ever forget that! They're just after one thing!

Ann's life had been filled with small petty details. Ordinary things. The days had rolled by unnoticed, safe and comfortable. When the suddenness caught up with her and she was thrown over the cliff, she wished that she'd been as candid as Charlotte. A woman who dared to show herself, dared to dress provocative and sexy. To stand up for women. Her feminine initiatives to life seemed to be the only solution. Now Ann wondered if Charlotte wasn't just preoccupied by her own things, what was she hiding behind those sexy curtains?

Take the men before they take you!
If I'm not sexy I don't have to stand the looks from men.

It was something here; she stopped in her train of thought and saw Mia's hands in front of her. Two apple halves that shall become a whole apple. The mystery of life, she thought and pulled carefully the quilt around her in bed. She would have a lay-in today. Let the world outside do as it pleased. She needed to land in her body, take back her female part.

Ann opened her eyes when she heard a key in the door. Charlotte?

Her stomach ached, she couldn't go back to school today. Why didn't she have a mother who cared like all the others? Last night she'd almost cried out due to the pain, and why hadn't her mother come? She'd barely made it into her bedroom. Yet, it had been David who half asleep had woken up. David wasn't even her real dad! With untidy hair he'd served her warm milk with honey. As if that would help! She'd had the stomach cramps on and off since New Year's Eve. She'd spoken to the school nurse several times. Nobody understood her, all the grown-ups were so busy and didn't listen to her. The school welfare officer wanted to know if she smoked and what job her mother had. What should she answer? That she had a mother who was a dipso and at the moment was together with David with the greasy face? It wasn't any point in getting hung-up on David, he could be replaced at any time. Filthy, worthless and alone – those were her last names. The last year in upper secondary school, who would she turn to after that? If she only could be like Charlotte.

Charlotte walks into the kitchen, fills a glass with mineral water. Why not two glasses? She puts it on the table next to the bed. Charlotte's transparent fading shell. Ann feels pity for her. An aching motherly feeling is spread from her chest and fills her, her eyes fill with tears. She imagines that the energy from her heart wells up and out through her eyes and tries to find their way into Charlotte, hoping it will give her some comfort.

Ann holds up the quilt.

Charlotte nestles down without hesitations. It's warm and cosy, it feels like home. They have known each other for such a long time, but she has never been this close to her. It's so unlike a man's hard body.

Soft.

Feminine.

Pliable.

Her hair has a faint scent of peach. She moves a little closer. Her hair tickles her nose. She takes her hand and moves her hair so the back of her neck becomes exposed. She stops an impulse to kiss that soft curve. Instead, she lets her hand caress her hair in slow strokes. She notices that Ann relaxes. It's so soft and quiet in the room and time seems to stand still. An existing. Without thinking of it, she has moved her body closer. Ann responds by pulling closer too. She lets her fingers follow her neck and feels the skin getting goose pimples under her fingertips. She leans forward and lets the tip of her tongue glide along her neck. Nibbles playfully on her ear lobe. Their bodies close in magnetically. The hand searches for the breasts. The stiff nipples want more. She slowly presses both breasts with her hands. They fit. Her lust to explore is great. Every part of her body shall be explored. They are so close. They know each other so well. She who's not like me but feels so true. A rhythm, without beginning, without an end.

PlayFul.

BlissFul.

SearchFul.

Pleasure. There is no time, no stress. No one who can see them, nobody who can hear them. Yet, everything feels superfluous present, like everything exists. As if they have always known, as if they belong together. Their hands seach over their bodies. They are both active. Sometimes Charlotte caresses, Ann receives. Nothing more or less. No guilt. No right or wrong. There's a rhythm in the flow. No musts, no plan. Bodies talking their own language, following the rhythm of nature.

They want more. Naked, entwined the boundaries start to fade. Their breathing has become faster. Aroused. The moist and the warmth. Their scent. Charlotte spreads Ann's legs. She gets closer with light fingers. Her vagina opens up. Feels the skin under her fingers. They're slowly getting closer. Caressing in circling moves. She sits up to see better. She's so beautiful down there. Like a bottomless bowl that awaits. Like a flower bud about to bloom. The soft skin on the inside of her thighs moves her on a spiritual level. Fingertips feel her skin. Ann responds, wants more.

No hurry. She feels the desire as much in herself as

she sees it in Ann. It's such a satisfaction. There is no time that can end. The next act has already begun before the foreplay has ended. Coherent fragments. Her fingers are getting closer to the clitoris. She knows what feels good. Cautiously searching closer. The moist down there, vanilla mixed with peach.

"Oh", the sound has formed an 'o' over her lips.

At the same time Ann has reached her feminine parts. It's wet. She's willing. They both are. Lower parts pressing against each other. Hands that touch. They love, they are one. One and the same.

"Something must die before something new can enter!"

Ann-Charlotte

Women are getting stronger out there, I can feel the power pulsate in the womb of Earth. A separation that once again becomes whole. Partial personalities that magnetically find thier way back to each other. Their time to heal is here. Tentative dance steps. The rhythm. Do you feel it? It lives. It's true. I feel it inside of me. It spreads. Floats away. Oceans are purified. Dried up rivers will once again flow in the shredding moon light. The sun will shine, and rills ripple louder than ever. Values will raise and get wings. New seeds will be sown with the wind. New plants will grow lushly. She feeds us. Gives us nourishment. It's already there. We are always welcome. We belong. We are. The train drives by unnoticed.

Ann-Charlotte took a few strong strokes away from the jetty. The dark water made her feel delight mingled with terror. The night swim was a threat to her own fear. She explored herself and did things she'd never dared before. Conflicting she ventured outside the safety she'd created around herself since her teenage years. The water bubbled around her body. Small tingling water bubbles that tickled. It started to rain. Small water dropped against the surface of the water. The cold was exactly what her brain needed. The questions started to cool down. Who was she really, the woman who swam alone here in the middle of the night? Who was she who tried to explore her deepest inner self?

With Charlotte by my side I have felt like an imprint, where I let everything flow through me. In my flexibility I let myself get lost by others' thoughts and feelings. The others took over to such a degree that I lost myself.

She crawled on, increased the tempo. Her breathing increased. It was a strain. She never used to swim out this far. She needed to explore her boundaries again. She could feel the characteristics as a part of herself. The natural and bold woman, Ann-Charlotte who she was, after all. Who was she today? Who? Questions that needed to be answered!

The pressure in her chest got worse. A twinge in her heart. She was in bad shape nowadays. She'd neglected her body, put it aside like an old mitten. Had let others decide when she needed to move her body. She had to take back the right to be in her own body. But not in the way women usually demanded: by getting angry or resolute.

We women must become better at loving our bodies.

In a responsible way, as an act of love to ourselves and to each other. She didn't really understand how, but it was okay not to know in the moment. She would know when it was time. She was on her way into a life that she'd never lived before. She wasn't what she'd been subjected to any longer. That had been brought out in broad daylight. The separation had healed. There was nobody who could desert her, but herself. That was what Mia had meant with responsibility, to react in full to life.

What if he isn't a he, but a she. What if she is me!

She slowed down and floated back towards the jetty. Her heart was beating hard and her breathing was strained. The fears of the dark water were gone, and she knew that she'd just begun a new phase. An end and a beginning of which she knew nothing. But it felt new and exciting. A tingling sensation. She cuddled up in bed, her hair was still wet. She was cold but didn't freeze. The smell of the cabin filled her, and the morning sun had already begun to peak in through the askew blind. The day was dawning outside. The new danced into her life. She fell asleep happy.

Bibbi

”You’re not going anywhere!”

”But I must be allowed to go outside.”

”Shut up!”

”Hell no!” She regretted her words before they had left her lips.

”Watch it! If you leave now you will never come in through that door again!” He clenched his fists.

A vein that looked like an earthworm throbbed in his forehead. She focused on that instead of his eyes. It moved. Pulsated.

He stood firmly in the doorway.

She was strong, but he was stronger. She would never be able to pass him. Powerless she sank to the floor. The nausea rose like a disgusting lump and mixed with her tears.

He looked satisfied. He stood still, contemptuously.

Wasn’t it that strength and the strong legs that she fell for? That first time that she’d returned to so many times. Her thoughts and feelings were mixed in an indefinable confused mess.

Who am I who sits here?

The thought popped up several times while his eyes seemed to penetrate her skin. She fought it. The vein pulsated. She remained sitting. He would win today again. She sunk further towards the floor. He jerked his head and left.

Loneliness pulled her down a deep black hole. At the same time, she wanted to run after him. Hold him. Caress him. Get him in a good mood again. But she stayed.

She must have sat still for a long time before the sleepiness fell over her. The light came in from the living room through the cracks in the wood. A few dust particles danced in the light, but everything else was quiet and still. Even the shoes stood properly still in rows. Motionless summer jackets hung on hangers. She went out to the very tidy kitchen. The first time she was here she'd thought it was gigantic. Endless counters that reached for the sea. How quickly one got used to things. He'd demonstratively left the dishes after dinner. She made a glass of squash. Her blood sugar was low. She hadn't eaten anything since lunch yesterday. She'd never had time to understand what had happened. All of a sudden, he'd come up behind her, he had been angry. Sulking because she was going out. The argument had started, even though she over and over again had assured him that she wasn't going anywhere, that she just wanted a breath of air. That wasn't forbidden, was it? In spite of her attempts to persuade him, his anger grew. She'd already gone too far. That was what he'd said. Gone too far?

She opened the door to the terrace and looked out over

the water. It would be a beautiful day. Maybe one of the last before the autumn would be more apparent. The chill in the air gave her goose bumps. She rubbed her forearms with her hands. She needed to book an appointment to wax them. He didn't like body hair. She tried to breathe in, but the air stopped like in an empty breath. Her lungs were pressed together, stuck like in a vice. Or a rusty old bucket full of holes. Something that couldn't be filled. A kind of convulsive difficulty in breathing. Her body was stiff after the strange sleeping position. She shook her head to get back to reality.

She would go inside and tidy up the kitchen. Take a hot bath and forget everything about yesterday.

Who was she to think that she was somebody!

Ann-Charlotte

Ann-Charlotte woke up with peace in her body. To wake up in the cottage every morning, to the sound of nature was like medicine to her. It was like she'd lived half of her life in forgetfulness. Inside of her there was an awakening going on. She had started to remember who she was. Did that sound weird? But when all her thoughts of flaws ended, she'd found a completion.

She pulled up the blind, what maybe was the last sparkling sun found its way over the broad floorboards.

The morning yoga that used to hang over her like a must was now a prolonged joy. A breath and she felt the warm air coming through her nose. On the inhale she felt a faint scent of soft soap. Yesterday she'd scrubbed the floor on her knees, inhaled the smell. A conscious act. Cleaned the narrow gaps between the floorboards. She had fetched bucket after bucket, until the water no longer had any colour.

She had cleaned over the years, vacuumed and swabbed. Every time they'd left the summer house it had been cleaned. There were memories of mountains of nappies, of baby bottles that had fell under the bed. Crayons that had found their way outside the paper. But this floor cleaning had been something else, an end of the summer. A reconciliation, a forgiving. A process in the presence. Her heart beat invitingly. Joined floorboards that created a foundation. A clean one. She let her hand stroke the planks. They'd been formed by feet in the life she had lived. The Sun Salutation.

Peeing dog. Yoga was a dance.

I am within myself with myself!

She pulled a dress over her naked body. The suntan was shaped around a swim suit, even the thin shoulder straps were marked in spite all attempts to pull them down. Her hair was sun-bleached and a few freckles had appeared on her nose. She looked several years younger than she'd done before the summer. Around her eyes the thin lines had become white after squinting in the sunshine. The sunglasses she'd worn for a long time, now lay inside on the chest of drawers in the hall. She wanted to see and experience all the colour changes. To be touched by life.

She studied the woman in the mirror. She seemed to soften a bit more every day. As if her skin made her body more round even though she didn't gain any weight. She didn't just look softer, but also more powerful. Her eyes were filled with vitality. She liked what she saw and smiled at her reflection. Took pity in all the years she'd hated her mirror image and all the harsh thoughts. Thoughts about flaws, you are wrong, ugly, fat.

She had lived a long time without being brave enough to show her feminine side. She'd done and did what she thought she had to do, that which she thought belonged to life. Then she had judged herself as a bad woman, mother and wife. And then had tried a little better. A little more.

She wasn't going to swim today. She'd taken her last swim yesterday, as a small ritual by herself. Her feet found their way through the grass and she could hear, but not see, the crickets sing. It was a new day; the morning chill didn't bother her, she loved to feel the dew against her feet. Brown-green grass tips swayed in the breeze. There were some yellow leaves under the birch. A few lonely leaves floated on the water. The water moved anxiously, as if it awaited something. Soon the wind would take hold of the reeds and raise it against the jetty. Twigs from the birch would be blown down by the wind. She would just rake them together in the spring. Or would she? Should she keep the summer house? Was there enough money for that?

She was surprised how easy it was to let the thoughts run off and for her to lose her newly found peace. The body wanted her to stay, but her thoughts and her analysing pulled at her.

The return to everyday life was a necessity. There were a lot of things she needed to sort out. The hermit would miss the changes of nature. Today she would return to the city, get back to her normal routine. How would that go? Feelings. Thoughts. It was all there. She was careful not to go any further with them. Took another deep breath. Breathed in for four seconds. Held her breath, counted to seven and slowly breathed out on eight. Mia had shown her that breathing technique. The rhythm with immediate effect.

You belong in the body, rest in your consciousness.

Everything was in order. The summer house was prepared for the autumn. The small rowing-boat was out of the water and lay on land. The oars were in the lake house. The ladder on the jetty was stowed away. But was she ready?

Ann-Charlotte went up to the house.

The days here had been precious, but also tough. The line she walked was thin. Stormy feelings could easily get their grip of her and make her fall headlong. The confusion she'd been living with the last years had disappeared. She slept well, even though she slept fewer hours. It was as if something was lurking all the time. Watched over her. Like a spider in its net. The time off from work had gotten her system to relax but there were still many loose ends that dangled in uncertainty of what they were going to be used for. Should she go back to taking patients and work as a couple's therapist?

The question came up several times a day, but she had no answer, and first she had to go back to work as a chambermaid at the hotel in the middle of the city.

Country versus city?

All memories from the summer cottage over the years had during the summer landed in her body, and she had sorted out the ones she wanted to keep. She had split them up in her memory bank in the save folder or the wastepaper basket. She glanced at the neighbour's house. She wished that she could wind back time and make a lot undone. But if she hadn't followed it through, she might not had ended up where she was now.

"Hey!" Ann-Charlotte flinched out of her deep thoughts. Tobias came jogging towards her. Him of all people!

"Hello."

"No morning swim today?"

He smiled self-confidently and pulled his hand through his hair. He was sweaty.

"I'm going back today."

He took a step closer. She wanted to flee. The agony crept under her skin and she started thinking about African worms that got under the skin and became visible. But he didn't seem to notice it and took another step closer. He stood so close that his sweat touched her skin. She felt the smell of fabric softener.

A shiver ran through her body and a feeling of wanting

him was mixed with aversion. Her body wanted it, she told herself. It was only her body that wanted it, like a teeming innocent animal. Something she couldn't help.

"How are you?"

She was surprised by his question.

"Fine, thank you! I'll go and do the rest of the packing. I guess you will continue your jogging?"

She locked her gaze at him. She was so ill-prepared for this. Wished that he had stayed away after the summer party. She'd even asked the angels for help. Something she'd done as a child when she wished that her mother would stop drinking.

Take care of Bibbi instead and let me be.

But he stayed. Let his eyes linger a bit too long on her shoulders. Then the breasts.

Didn't he get it?

She looked demonstratively towards his house and thought she saw Bibbi. For a moment it felt as if she looked up at her and their eyes met over the long distance. The seconds passed by, it was pulsating between them. She wasn't an animal, she was a human being. After what seemed like forever, she managed to gain control. He jogged away.

Her legs were heavy on their way back to the house. She sank down on the sofa. The same sofa had been there all the years. A grey one from Ikea. With a few simple moves it turned into a sofa bed. One of the handles were broken and she poked at it with her foot. The memories in the house. The family life was pressing onto her. Even though she'd cleared away several rooms there were still memories left from times gone by. A family. A home. Happy suntanned children that played. Tears she thought had dried a long time ago welled up.

She wasn't prepared for the fact that she would react so strongly. The years had shaped her, she fell so easily into her old feelings again. Now she'd let Tobias pull her down because of something she'd done. She was ashamed over herself before Bibbi.

Tobias had entered in a phase of her life when she needed sex. She heard how bad that sounded. But she couldn't blame Charlotte any more, or that which she had been subjected to. Only she and nobody else was responsible.

She didn't want Bibbi to find out. What if she already knew! She felt uneasy. A feeling of not being free got hold of her. Pulled her down. She wanted to defend herself. It was he who had been unfaithful, not her. He had encouraged her.

Then he came jogging over her garden like a muscular alpha male on her path! Anger tore in her.

Who did he think he was?

Mia

Mia welcomed Ann-Charlotte with a radiant smile. Her heartiness spread like heating crystals over Ann-Charlotte's whole body and her eyes were filled with tears. Since she'd let herself be touched by life, she felt more.

"Something has happened to you, there's a visible change!" Mia's eyes looked into her, through all layers. She had to admit that the piercing gaze used to make her feel insecure, as if she should have felt guilty for something but not knowing what for. That made her remember who she was: free, beautiful and natural. Just splendid.

She followed Mia through the lived-in apartment, weaved her way through the furniture. Undreamt-of possibilities seemed to wrap themselves around her, old dreams came to life every time she met Mia. Yet tangible tranquil in her presence. The ego quieted and all noise felt distant.

It was Mia who'd helped her find her way back to her previous lost separated part. Weeks after the fusion she had felt euphoric. Thankful.

When the separation in her healed, her whole experience changed.

"I kind of just *am* right now. I don't need anything. Don't miss anything."

"When we let our thoughts and feelings be as they are, just let them be there as any bird in the tree, our thoughts find peace. A natural state."

When I experience myself as whole, I lack nothing.

"You have done an enormous job!"

She had to admit that too: when she changed old ingrained conceptions, the world became clearer to her and she felt whole. To have lived in separation since her teens had cost her a lot of suffering. Stomach pains. Many sleepless nights. The separation had been the foundation for her whole adult life. With that in her luggage she had created tiresome and torn relationships. Guilt. Frustration. But she had not known. She had thought that if she changed her ways, if she only became a little better, everything would feel different. A pattern which she, the past year, had ransacked. Well-tried old ideas didn't work in the new. With a long marriage behind her she could see that she'd been living in a state of dreams. Had created a world to keep her conceptions alive. Thanks to the divorce from Samuel she could heal and take back the separated part.

"The guilt we carry is separation. We have split ourselves from the whole."

"It sounds obvious when you say it! As if it makes me remember who I am, my origin."

It's quiet for a while.

"I feel reborn! But also terrified of losing the new." Ann-Charlotte drinks some water.

"What happens if you lose it?"

"I will fall back into the old that I'm used to."

"Now you're back up in your head! What happens if you lose it?"

"I'll separate myself from me again. And I'll experience guilt."

"Aha!"

"The image I get is that I stand on the top of a hill. I know that I have to jump, but not what will happen. I don't know what it will look like down there."

Ann-Charlotte saw the metaphor in front of her. Remembered the nightmares.

"What happens if you step into that woman?"

"I can get hurt, threatened, violated."

"What happens if you step into that woman?"

Ann-Charlotte took a deep breath. Exhaled loudly and ordered her body to relax. It fought her. She took a new breath. Mia put her hands on her stomach. It was down there she was going. Down to the bottom. Deep inside her womb. A memory of Cayla in her womb flickered by. She tried to get hold of it, but the memory marched past like a fast train. A new attempt. Inhale and exhale. She could hear Mia talk. She sounded firm. Even if she knew that Mia wanted to support her to take one step forward, it felt like a threat, as if she would push her over the cliff. She just wanted to run away from there. Separate herself from the feeling. The guilt filled her. All the mistakes she'd made. Everything she could have done better.

"Who are you who are free to follow your own way?"

"Who are you who dare being the woman in your life?"

"What happens in you now?"

Deeper down.

Inwards.

An illogical pattern.

Guilt.

Anger.

"It feels like I will die, if I let myself live as the magnificent woman that I am, I will die!"

Her legs felt heavy, it would be impossible to take a single step from here. She was frozen to the spot. The guilt took its grip on her. Shame over her life. The life she hadn't lived. Wasn't she as free as she thought? Earlier in life she had fought to not become as her mother. Not the type of woman that stood bitter by the stove. But in the struggle, she became someone else, not what she was destined to be. Instead she'd become what she had thought she needed to be. Another type of untrue woman. The guilt was handed down: one big collective DNA of co-dependent women. All of them were untrue. Relationships that were held together by guilt and slowly pulled them under despise and hatred.

Separation – guilt – judgement.

It was time to take a step into the new without reserva-
tion. Take the step. When she was ready to stretch out her
leg and take the step, the road would be visible. She would
walk, others would follow.

Bibbi

Tobias went straight towards me, looked into my eyes and asked if I used to come here often. I couldn't help myself from laughing. That old classic line. Now we were at a sportswear trade fair. My brother had invited me. I remember that I thought of love at first sight. After that I had lost sight of him, but a couple of weeks later he turned up unannounced behind me at a party.

"Hi, do you often come here?"

I felt it in the whole of my body. As if something came to life in me.

I will have a baby with him!

He's the one!

He encouraged me. He listened and asked questions, was interested in me on a deep level, like no one else had been before.

It was like we knew each other. It sounds like a worn phrase, I know, but it was as if we were one. Destiny had brought us together. He was the man I'd been waiting for my entire life. There was a fire in me, finally!

We said goodbye that night under a street light. A romantic kiss. My body was on fire, but I didn't want to fail and go to bed with him on the first date. Ruin all that was beautiful. I'm not like that.

I'd just got indoors when I got the first text message.

I can't manage without you, I want you close!

I think it was that 'close' I fell for, but I didn't answer, just sat down on the floor there in the hall. Moved by the night. Happy, excited, but also afraid.

Would I be good enough for him?

Was I good enough?

Good looking enough?

He was perfect. Fit. Muscular. What if I was the only one thinking like this? What if this was a bad movie and he got hit by a car on his way home?

And then he just stood there outside my door. Took me in his arms when I opened it. Carried me into the living room. Lay me down on the sofa and looked at me. Just looked, let his gaze undress me. I had lost words. Then we made love. I have never done it before on the first date. Had heard that it wouldn't be perfect, that it takes time to find the rhythm together. I was seen! He courted me as if he knew what to do. It was like we'd met before. He knew my body. Orgasms – I lost count of them. A long climax of shared connection. He satisfied me, said he enjoyed doing it. He couldn't get enough, me neither. We slid off the sofa, down onto the floor. We made love until I hit my head on the wall on the other side of the room. We laughed at it. We slept together. The bonds between us were strong, we stayed almost all day in bed. Just us. Inseparable. When we were going to part it was like a purgatory. We both cried.

He was married but said: "Give me a week."

But the weeks passed. He argued about the apartment. I was on my way to leave him many times. But I loved him, he was my everything. I didn't think I was a woman who could be together with a man like him. But time passed. Then he sent in the divorce papers. It was just us.

She starred at the water that whirled down in the sink. She would like to whirl down there, disappear. Dissolve and return to an empty state of endless water. The unbearable thirst had its grip on her. She drank from her hand. The water iced on its way down to her stomach, that contracted. For a moment she thought it would come up again. Her hands were ice-cold, and she put them on her head to cool it down, one on her forehead, one in the nape of her neck. Breathe, she thought. Breathe through this. Deep breaths. She forced herself to stay. The pictures flicked before her eyes.

Cautious exploration after the argument. New tastes. New moves, yet so in sync. But she didn't want to make love to him. She was afraid there would be more blood. After the last intercourse she'd called the midwife. It could happen early in a pregnancy. Yes, it had only been a few streaks on the toilet paper but had been enough to scare her. He'd been rough on her, pulled her hair back and spread her legs.

She looked in the mirror. The waterproof mascara didn't deliver on its promise. The eyelids were swollen. Her nostrils had red spots. She couldn't do this any longer. The whole week she'd been bothered by her nausea. Nothing seemed to help. Maybe it would go away after she had told Tobias, as the midwife had said. But how? Her plans always derailed. What was she afraid of? She pulled a hand through her hair.

She wanted to keep the baby, she knew that much. But all her incomprehensible thoughts – the nausea made it hard to make something out of them. She vomited for the second time. Washed her face and rubbed it with the hand lotion she had in her handbag. That felt better. If it was like the last few weeks had been, the feeling of sickness would stay away for a while now. She took some ice-cold water in her mouth, gargled and spat it out. She left the customer bathroom. She imagined that she was like any other pregnant woman while she pushed the trolley down the isles. She put in things that she randomly remembered Tobias had mentioned. Between the shelves with cleaning agents she was taken by surprise with the nausea. She threw up in her handbag.

She thought she saw a curios gaze in the shop assistant's eyes when she hurried back to the toilet. She rinsed her handbag out. It was an expensive incident.

The same procedures. Ice-cold water on her forehead. Vomiting. Gargle with water. The only difference was that she didn't have the strength to look at herself in the mirror. She just wanted to go home now. Have time to sleep for a while before he got home.

She sat for a while in the car with the door open. Listened to the sounds. The crickets. Did she hear the sea as well, or was it just imagination?

She carried the bags inside. Put the dairy products in the fridge and lay down on the bed cover.

Shouldn't she be happy over the fact that she was pregnant?

Ninth week, womb the size of an orange, the midwife had told her. She put her hand on her belly.

Give me strength, power and courage to tell.

She slept until she heard a key in the door.

"Hello?"

When Tobias stood by the bed, she knew that she wouldn't tell him today either.

"Oh, I must have fallen asleep."

"Are you sick?"

"No, I don't think so. I went to the shop and just got so tired."

"I thought it smelled like vomit in the hall."

She remembered the handbag.

"Are you hungry?"

"Yes, a little."

"Do you want me to make you an omelette?"

"Mm, with lots of onion."

"With a lot of onion? Okay. Fixing it."

He disappeared to the kitchen. She realized that it had darkened outside. She'd slept the whole day away. She hoped she could sleep during the night and not have to lie and worry over how she should form the words.

I'm pregnant!

You will be a father.

We're having a baby!

Hey, I'm pregnant!

What did one say?

Bibbi sometimes found herself missing the lit lamp in Ann-Charlottes cottage, she thought when she sat down at the table. From up here the house looked smaller than it was. Everything seemed further away. After the summer party she and Ann-Charlotte had started to talk to each other. First a little cautiously, but then a little deeper. They had much in common. Or was it just those things that bound women together?

Tobias stepped straight into the pile of clothes to reach the towel. The water was still dripping from him when he wrapped it around his body. He was in good shape. He flexed his muscles in a pose. Scrutinized himself in the mirror.

Just like a self-absorbed teenage boy, she thought. What will he think about her body changing? The belly that would grow for another thirty weeks. She would be more of a woman, more adult. She saw the picture of Mother Earth in front of her. Rounded hips. Full breasts.

"We need to talk!"

"I'm tired now. Why don't you call me tomorrow at lunch?"

When did she become a phone call over lunch? This was about their unborn child. She needed support in this. She couldn't possibly sleep. She patted up in her dressing gown. She leaned her forehead against the window. The cold spread over her brow. She placed her hands over her stomach. Then she took her phone and sent a text to Ann-Charlotte. It was after eleven, but she would understand.

Ann-Charlotte

She went round the corner of the hotel and walked faster towards the staff entrance. She was late the first day after the holiday. Her morning routines had taken longer than usual, and she'd got used to live without stress. Back as a chambermaid. A small detour on her main road. She didn't know the rest of the road, but right now she was here. The fifty-year-old who had put her career aside to do something else. Not a smashing headline. Now she just hovered between different possibilities.

She had told herself to wait and see what the division of her and Samuel's joint property would lead to, and then stabilize her finances before she moved on. Then there was a dream of going on a trip to an exciting continent. There was a distant wish of meeting a new man. But the future was uncertain, and she often dreamt of spending the rest of her life on her own. Maybe move into the summer house for good and live every day as it came. There were many questions, she thought when she opened the door to the staff room. It was empty, except for a note that welcomed her back and said that she was supposed to go up to the third floor. She quickly changed into her work uniform and hurried up.

”Hi, did you have a good time?” Maija didn't wait for an answer and took some extra pillowcases from the cart and ran into a room. Ann-Charlotte let her gaze move over her colleagues who were hurrying in and out of the rooms. Except for that, the corridor was quiet. The lights had gone out and no one had bothered to turn it on again. She pushed the switch with the red lamp. For how long would the lights be turned on? Long enough for a guest to have time to get to the right room. Some of the new girls she yet had not met giggled at something. She wanted to say hello, but the tempo was high, nobody noticed her. The bookings the upcoming weeks were high, she saw that on the room cleaning list. She did what she was supposed to and fell into the tempo. At lunch she had a cup of coffee and went out to sit down. Personnel from the kitchen made room for her at a shabby plastic table that once had been white. She needed to breathe, be alone, but yet sat down on the wobbly plastic chair. Someone had lit a cigarette and she longed for the fresh smell of the sea. A half-hour long lunch break. She already missed the freedom. Contrasts. It was mixed feelings, but some way or another she managed to live through the day. She sent a couple of text messages to Bibbi.

Even if the tiredness was there and the confusion at times came as a complete fact, she felt satisfied when she went home. On Mia's advice she had welcomed all thoughts, even the ones she before had deemed as 'bad'. She leaned back against the wall. Behind all this there were people who she knew, experienced. They lived. Went to work. Felt guilt, joy and happiness. That, inside the houses, allured her. The curiosity. As a child she had tried to see who lived behind the walls. Fantasized. Imagined.

Life is like a dream, an illusion.

When she got older, she'd created happy images behind the house fronts. Sometimes when Samuel had been driving, she'd looked up at the walls and dreamt of the rich people who had a happy and good morning. An early morning. Families that were still in bed. Small children running to their tired parents. A cephalopod with unproportionable eyes. The parents' sneaking attempts to find some time for nude play with each other while the children's programme was on.

All of a sudden, she was back in her old life. In the big and safe home of her family. A relaxed Saturday morning before the day's agenda started. A children's party, where's the gift? Was I supposed to buy that? I thought you said ... Who will drive Cayla to the stable? Shit, the match is on the other side of Greenville ... Simon, wake up! The everyday stress that started after a somewhat longer lie-in. That life had been worth so much. Her life. She hadn't realized it then, not known that time eventually would run away. That it would be quiet to wake up. Quiet to come home. She missed the family. That which they had created together. The helix whirled. She continued on the road. Didn't notice the man that slowed down and looked at her. He looked at her from head to toe with an appreciating smile. Neither did she notice that she was on her way to walk into another stressed man. He, who in spite of his irritation eyed her. The dress she wore was old, but of a more exclusive brand. Bought in London. They'd once just decided to go there over a weekend. She and Samuel. A weekend with no children. As usual it had been a bit tense. That feeling that had always been in their relationship: 'if-I-get-too-close-to-you, I'm-disturbing-you'-feeling with Samuel. They had started to fuss over something. She didn't remember what. It was some small detail in the evening before they went out for dinner. She'd just wanted to curl up in bed and fall asleep. He'd been waiting impatiently for her at the hotel pub. They ate a quiet dinner. He drank his beer in big gulps. He always did that when he was upset. She'd imagined another togetherness and that they would make love. He fell asleep with his back towards her. Yet, she'd said that it had been her happiest weekend when they got home.

Her thoughts had spun off and she stopped at a street corner to catch her breath. Was it her ego that created all this? To make her feel guilty and bad? She breathed in and counted 4/7/8.

When she got closer to the house, she saw a parked car.

She cautiously opened the front door. It was as if she knew that the visit was hers even though she didn't recognize the new car. Couldn't believe her eyes when her mother and David smiled at her. She looked at them. She must have looked very surprised.

"Hi", David said with a big smile.

"Hello, hello. What are you doing here?"

"Hi, honey." Her mother's raucous voice pulled her back. She had always been ashamed of her, ashamed over the smell of cigarettes. Now she saw that her mother's eyes were smiling, there was a tingle she'd never seen before. She hugged them both.

David smiled at her and winked flirtatiously.

"Will you offer us some coffee?" He blinked once more, and his gold tooth glistened.

"Sure, it's nice that you're here!" She meant it, even if she was longing for a hot shower.

"You look so nice in that dress!" Her mother smiled. Ann-Charlotte was astonished by the fact that the whole world could be so different since she'd let herself be more herself. She was supported and encouraged as a woman by others in a new way. As if she had support. That which she had tried to get before by demands, now came easily to her, often unexpectedly.

Unlike most of the others, she had thought that the start of a new term was the best. Now she would be away from home during the days. Even if she had to pretend like her life was normal, school was still a free zone to her. She liked to listen to others telling about their trips abroad and car trips with whining siblings. Maybe it would always be her dream to experience a real family holiday?

Her relation to her mother had been laced with bottles of alcohol. The memories of her mother's love were worn. She had tried to remember sympathy and love, but in vain. Instead, she remembered numerous men that had been there and then disappeared. Tim with the knife. Martin. She didn't know much about her own father. David had stayed the longest. But she'd been ashamed of his teeth and oily skin. He had once taken her to a pet shop. It was like a zoo, but for free, he'd said.

”What's the name of that?” She'd pointed at a fish with a wide mouth.

”*Silurus glanis,* also called catfish.”

After that she had called him Catfish.

The coffee tasted good. Right now, she didn't want to think about all the cups of coffee that she had gulped down during the day. She would have difficulties sleeping, but she also had a lot to process. The whole day had been like observing, studying herself. The scene had been almost the same the whole day. The chores the same, but inside of her the tones of life had been played. She was happy with the day. To listen and be affected was the new theme of her life.

236

That was something new, now that she sat here with her mother and David. For the first time in her adult life she realized that she could let her mother be who she was. She accepted her and tried not to get her attention or change her. Compassion? An understanding on a holy, deeper level? As if she was done trying to get the mother she'd never had. But from now on she could be the daughter she was meant to be.

"You look so knowing. Are you up to something?"

"Oh, we do?" David pretended to look surprised at her mother and blinked. The same blink he'd had when she was six years old and they were on their way to the cinema for the first time. The social welfare payed.

"Yes, I thought you might drive us home." She put the keys in her hands. "In your new car."

"What?" She sat absolutely still for a moment. The images of her cruising to the summer house got a new dimension. The world opened up. She threw herself into her mother's arms. Tears were pouring out of both of them. Gratitude filled her heart.

Bibbi

The days were spent on holding her head over the surface and at night she was tossed into inexplicable long thoughts. She hadn't told Tobias about the pregnancy. The weeks went by. She was quiet. Because she already knew that he didn't want any children. He wouldn't like that her body changed. He didn't think that women should breastfeed because that ruined their breasts. They were a woman's gift to the man. She'd heard him say that several times. She'd started to feel aversion against him. He grabbed her like he owned her. She was so much more. A woman, not an unworthy sex object. Her shame was turning into anger. Towards all men that saw women as objects. Their eyes that helped themselves to the treat in front of them. Men like Tobias with a way that made the woman feel that she wasn't good enough, not beautiful enough. A subtle energy, gazes that lingered. Eyes that moved over a woman's body. A look that stayed on her hips and breasts. She'd never got used to their looks. She didn't like it. When Tobias sent signals to other women, even she was affected. It was also the men's task to screw the woman as if she begged for it. That was how she'd heard him explain it on several occasions. She'd been one of those women who'd begged, but without knowing it. All she sought was love. Now that she was pregnant she started to see things clearer. Did she want her child to have a father who screwed other women?

She was tired. From afar she heard Tobias banging angrily with the pots in the kitchen. They had argued again. She closed her eyes. Weariness fell over her and she drifted into subconscious dreams.

It was a bitterly cold winter. The cold held its grip over the valley. The famine was the worst in many years. Everyone did what they could for a piece of bread. People were starving. The air vibrated of worry and a flock of waxwings fled at the sound of a ringing bell. The farmhand manages the horse with a firm hand. Its warm breath creates small clouds. The animal works hard in the newly fallen snow and the sweat lathers on its shoulders. The sleigh glides safely and steady.

"Whoa!"

The driver pulls the reins and the horse obediently stops in front of a cottage. The man's fur coat reaches down to the snow and creates a track on his way to the house, where he knocks on the door. With the force of his body he pushes it open. The horse nervously scrapes with a hoof. The sisters lie listless on the floor. The smaller one hangs with her head. Their scanty and worn clothes almost falling off of them. The caps in green wool are mothy and their cardigans made in the same yarn are filled with holes. One of the children has stuck its finger in one of the holes and nervously twists the yarn without knowing it. That's the only movement in the room. With a resolute face the man lifts the girls and carries them, one on each side of his body. Weak and cold: there is no resistence, even though their mother has told them never to go with a stranger. But there's something wrong with mother. She's cold and blue where she lays in her bed.

A blanket is wrapped around them and the package is placed on a sheep's skin. They are hardly alive when the little bell starts to ring again, and even less aware of where they are going.

The next time they wake up it is warm. They embrace each other. Their eyes are closed, the older sister moves her hand over the fabric beneath her. She's never felt anything like it. It's soft and smooth but also warm and cool at the same time. It sounds like there's a crackling fire, but she doesn't have the strength to open her eyes. She carefully squeezes her sister's hand. Her mouth is filled with a sweet beverage. She makes a smacking sound when it goes down her throat. Sometimes she hears her sister's heavy breathing before she falls into lethargy again. There is no worry any more. Not for her or her sister. Soon mother will come as well. Everything is just so nice and warm, and she doesn't mind staying in her sleep.

Muffled voices, as if they are far away, she can sense them but not hear the words. The voices touch her body. Rub her body with something, a scent she doesn't recognize. One day she has the strength to open her eyes for a moment and she sees her sister next to her. Next time she moves her hand and strikes a strand of hair from her sister's face. They are alive.

She pretends to be asleep when the beverage is given to her. She can clearly hear the words now. Even if she cant't understand all that was said, because they're talking about other people, names she doesn't know. Difficult names, like rich people.

"Look, just skin and bone on the poor ones. It'll take time for them to feed up!" The voice sounds a little harsh from the woman with bigger hands and deeper voice.

The other voice is a bit softer and has soft tender hands. "Yes, look at the little one also. But it looks like it's turned now. It's so awful that they've lost their mother."

The words stay with her and make her tired, but they are still there when she wokes up. Motherless!

Did that mean that mother had left them to find food or work? As soon as she gets her strength back she will find her. The last thing she remembered from the cottage was the cold, the short green string of wool yarn her sister had been sucking on, even if it had made her rough around her lips. She just has to find their clothes when it is time to look for their mother. First, her little sister needs to get her strength back. She isn't awake as often and they have only looked into each other's eyes a few times. She's so thin. Her skin is transparent and the blue veins against the white skin look ghostly. Her eyelids close and the picture of her tired sister changes into dreams. They are always the same. Before the cold, before the hard times. When father worked, and mother stood by the wood stove. She never dreams about that other, that which happened after their father disappeared. About the men who came and went when mother stayed in bed and the girls had to do everything. Until it got too cold.

***

The day had been long. Her body ached but the work for the day wasn't over yet. The soft soap smelled nice on the kitchen floor. She let the scouring-cloth suck up the dirty water and moved the zinc bucket. She let her hands rest for a while in the water. The soap heals rough hands. Her knees ached and rubbed against the wooden floor. Her arms didn't work with the same intensity as before, the muscles felt short and tight. The only sound that was heard was from the scrubbing-brush. She continued to scrub, the monotone sound made her remember a lullaby. That was all she remembered of her mother. The brush slowly glided back and forth, she held it with both hands. The images from the day passed by. She'd got up early to peel the potatoes. She'd carried silver trays and served. Everything had run as planned and both the matron and the housefather should be pleased. She should feel more grateful for her work. If it hadn't been for ... She pushed the thoughts away, she would try to accept what was coming to her. After all, she got out of the kitchen and got to be around the guests. The white blouse was too tight, and the short skirt hampered her in her work. She stretched her back. She had sent her sister to bed a long time ago, she was so pale. Her concern for her fragile sister always lay as a shadow over her. She stretched and rubbed her hips, the pain stabbed and stung. The day had been long and she wanted to take off her shoes and lie down.

She took the bucket and locked the kitchen door. She looked at the mansion that was quiet. She poured the water over some willow herbs when she passed the hen house on her way home. She could sense the rooster's wish to come out, he who's life meaning was to tell them about

242

the new day. She hadn't minded when the mistress of the house had asked them to move back to the cottage. Even if it meant more struggle for them both, especially with her sister's pale face. She earned her coins to afford medical treatment. She had also heard about a woman with herbs who lived in the forest. Maybe she should turn to her instead? The carriage alone to the doctor would cost a fortune.

When she was out of sight she bent down and took off her shoes. Not only her feet ached, but also her legs all the way up to her hips. Her little toe was bleeding and she had several blisters. Despite that, it felt nice to walk barefoot, the pine needles were like balm. All of a sudden, she didn't feel tired. The smells of summer came to her. The birds were busy feeding their chicks. She picked some blueberries and wished she'd had a bowl to put them in to take some home to her sister. The next day off she would bring her here to pick some. They could dry them for the winter, like their mother had always done. She was stabbed with pain when she thought about their mother. A feeling of vengeance crept under her skin. She understood that it wouldn't be good to live with the bitterness. But she'd heard the words being whispered around her:
"Obscure woman!"

She hurried on to get a few hours' sleep. She saw the cottage in the distance. Their dwelling. A ramshackle house, but it was a home. The door was open. Was her sister already awake? She stepped up her pace and suspected something was wrong. She let go of her shoes and ran towards the open door. She sensed that something wasn't right. She felt it in her stomach. She stopped at the threshold. Her eyes followed the walls. She saw signs of tumult. Blankets and parts of the sparse furnishing was thrown on the floor. What had happened? She was on her way to call out, but something told her not to. She had to follow her instinct, as she'd done so many times lately. She strategically looked for signs of where her sister could be. She lifted blankets and looked at all hiding places she could think of. Once they had both fitted into that firewood bin. They had curled up in it to seek protection.

The anger got hold of her. The fatigue was gone. Old feelings tore inside of her. The men who had started to sneak around the cottage. She glanced repeatedly at the door. The other night she herself had aimed a thick stick at a sturdy man. He had fled.

"Damn you, bloody syphilis kids!" He had panted and protected his head and ran.

The word syphilis had bored into her and given her a furious strength. Their mother had died of syphilis that cold winter day when death was on their threshold. Infected by men! The mother had carried the blame and they inherited it.

She must find her sister, who was weak and feeble and could hardly defend herself. Where could she have gone? Had something happened to her? She tried to think strategically while she made up quick plans of revenge. She took the cast-iron frying pan. Let her fingers follow the beam next to the mantelpiece. Yes, there was the hidden knife. She'd sharpened it recently. She went out. There had to be some signs. Instinctively as a dog she stopped outside and smelled the air. She slowly walked east of the house towards the forest. Her pupils expanded. Suddenly she saw an inner picture of her sister being hunted by two men. There was a marsh further up and a boulder with a cave-

like hiding place where they had used to play as children. She saw this in her mind and moved on. She walked over stones and bushes almost noiseless. Her skirt had slid up and sat on her hips. In one hand the frying pan gleamed, she held the knife in the other. She was determined to find her sister. They had developed a telepathic power between each other and she could feel her sister showing the way.

She heard voices. Slowed down and crept slowly. Two robust men's backs. She heard her sister whimper, could feel the pain from her feminine lower parts. Damned whoremongers! She was about to throw herself at them and stab the knife into one of them but stopped herself. She had to be cunning. If she got hurt ... Two strong men. She didn't have the strength. They were strong and well-fed. They would soon walk pass her hiding place behind the tree. Her brain worked on finding a quick solution. Her heart pounded hard in her throat. She could hit one of them with the pan and stab the other one with the knife. But if she didn't succeed hitting the man to the ground? He was tall, she needed to hit hard on his head.

She sank down in the moss. Her hands were shaking and she let go of the objects. She looked at her hands. She was not a murderer! She went up to her sister. She was unconscious. It smelled of blood and she was pale. Her pulse was very weak. Carefully, as if the sister was a porcelain doll, she carried her to the marsh. Washed her. She tore shreds from her white serving blouse. Blood from her sister's vagina dripped down in the soil, disappeared into the moss. The smell of the men filled her eyes with tears. She tried frantically but carefully to wash the smell away. She washed her until the only scent she could smell was meadow flowers and the marsh's delights. She carried her sister to another place. She would sneak back to the cottage and get some things. They weren't safe there. They had to get away as soon as her sister could move again ...

She woke up with a start. Her body felt ill-matched, like severed limbs. She hovered between now and the dream. A new unfamiliar feeling. She opened her eyes. The light was dim. The woolen blanket rubbed her skin like blunt needles. Tens of thousands of needles. The same green colour as the mothy clothes. Her hand searched its way down to her lower parts. No, she wasn't bleeding. The hand on her stomach. It was still there. She could clearly feel the hard lump that was her womb. The dream had been so real. The sisterhood. The contempt from the men. The woman's struggle. She came to think of Ann-Charlotte. Lately, she had felt a strong kinship between them. Meeting on a deep level. Sometimes the words weren't even needed. Female intuition.

Now she knew, she would leave Tobias!

She stomped unnecessarily hard when she put her feet on the floor, as to force her not to change her mind. She would venture out on the journey of her life, explore life as a woman. She would start to listen to her inner voice and follow it. Dance with life. When she did that, women from the past would not have suffered in vain. The force filled her.

The Divine Mother

Ann-Charlotte breathed out. She saw a mental image of her summer house. The path she took daily down to the water. Her naked feet knew where every blade of grass grew. Every little rock and curve. It was her path of life. The path that held her alive. A feeling in a universe she knew. A place on Earth. She saw herself walk on the path of the soul surrounded by beautiful nature. A beautiful woman. She felt the ground holding her and she looked up at the tree tops. She stopped and turned around. The path split in two. A crossroad. Mother, it said on one road sign. She followed the path with her inner sight. The genetic make-up lay like long molecular courses with genetically transferable information. Everything was stored. Aware of the heritage she'd inherited from her mother, grandmother, great grandmother ... The chain was indefinite. Women who had given birth to children. There were women who had fought. The road was laced by personal destinies. There was a view of women from the men around them. They pulled her back, wanted her to fight. Stand up in the struggle!

She lost her strength and slumbered in a dumb state. She slipped in the mud and twitched. Reality became tangible. Her head spun when she opened her eyes.

It was time to stop fighting, it was time to find a balance between the woman and the man.

I remember my origin.

I remember who I am.

I make place for the divine immense power.

Doubts and fears fall off of me.

The struggle is over.

I don't need to fight for my right to be who I am destined to be any more.

Everything is perfect.

Samuel

He remembered so much these days, that which he before took for granted. All that he was used to had new proportions. He felt hatred and love. Could he really be in contact with both at the same time? He wanted to beat back time. Punched hard at his ego. Unspeakable feelings fought within him. But the days passed by, all the same; his eyes scanned the same papers at the office. The constant hum from the computer. The same practised workout at the gym. But he did it. He stayed above the surface. Cayla now slept at her boyfriend's house. Simon at his. The house echoed empty when he came home.

That's why he called Fanny, he told himself. To lighten the weight in his chest. A soft willing body that made him forget. But tonight, he would tell her that he couldn't go on. It had been three weeks since last time. And she continually asked. Demanded! Wanted to have a child. Start a family.

No, it was a clear and definite no.

Start all over when life finally lay in front of him. Or behind him. He looked mournfully in the mirror. The grey hairs had replaced the previous so lively curls. He should shave off all his hair. Be like the fire fighter models with cute puppies in the calendars. He flexed his muscles. He wasn't out of shape, but far from a superman.

He was a tired man who didn't want any more children. But wouldn't be like Ann-Charlotte: from orderly businesswoman to hippie. He would do something great in life. Maybe start a company, become an agent of some sort. Earn money and move to another country. Write a book.

He would start by thanking Fanny, it wasn't fair to her that he engaged half-heartedly in their relationship and had used her to forget his ex. She wanted a real relationship. To have children. Nagged about the fact that they'd been seeing each other for over a year. Women could have demands too. He'd heard how men talked in the changing room.

"How's your ex?"

"You mean my sex!"

They had laughed. But the laughs had sounded false.

He wasn't going to break up over the phone or with an e-mail. He would do it face to face like a real man. She immediately answered his text message. She would come in the evening. Fanny would probably cry, he had to endure that. The following week he was going to contact Ann-Charlotte to sell the summer cottage. It wasn't good for her to be there all by herself. It probably wouldn't take long before a man came and took her. He also needed the money.

She breathed heavily. In, out. The pain showed in her

face. Her eyes were tightly shut. The baby was in the wrong position. Didn't get enough oxygen. He heard the doctor's words in the back of his head. Different alarms were lit at the delivery ward. Signals. Something is wrong. The midwife's anxious face but comforting words. "Usually, it goes well." He has to fix this. Whatever it means, he has to stay strong by her side. We must get through this, he thought while the hospital bed was rolled into the elevator.

She was beautiful, Fanny. Her soft healthy skin under his fingers. Youthful. Sporty. What was she doing with an old man? Sure, he had some experience. He was a good lover, but his stamina and heart weren't there. She should have someone who could give her all that. She deserved it like any other woman. He embraced her, inhaled the scent of her hair. She smelled fresh. Not old, musty summer cottage or sour breast milk. He couldn't even get fully committed in the embrace, Ann-Charlotte was still in his thoughts. It was her smell he missed. It had been the two of them.

The children's rucksacks were packed with water and snacks. They wore caps as sun protection. Ann-Charlotte had hugged them at least a hundred times when they saw the Peugeot driving up along the road.

"Look, here's Granddad!"

Simon's shoe lace was loose again, and Ann-Charlotte bent down to tie it, but Simon thought it was another hug.

He hugged her, and his weight knocked her over and they landed with a thump on the grass. They both laughed happily. Ann-Charlotte was just up on her feet again.

"I also want to do that with you, Mum!"

Ann-Charlotte had to do it three times before Cayla was satisfied.

"Hello, hello, what are you doing if I may ask?" His mother took off her sunglasses.

Ann-Charlotte wore Simon's cap backwards on her head and tried to brush off the grass. In moments like these he felt like he'd chosen his wife carefully to get away from his mother's stiffness. His mother, who was small, slender-limbed and made to be put on a pedestal. Somewhere deep within he knew that it was that meticulous streak he was worried that Cayla had inherited.

Samuel embraced his mother unwillingly. He had a feeling that he wasn't good enough for her.

"You look amazing, Mum! And a newly washed car, as usual, Dad." He liked him. He was simple and straight on. The children loved him.

"Jump in, kids. This is the taxi to the zoo!"

Simon admired his grandfather and was quick to get inside the car. Cayla had to hug a couple of times more before she installed herself. Within a few minutes the car drove off. It would be quiet without them, he noted. They started to go up to the house when the car was out of sight.

"Does your father never get tired of washing their car?"

252

"Maybe not."

"Don't ever be like that!"

He pulled her closer. Kissed her lasciviously. She answered half-heartedly. Yet, a small feeling of disappointment started to take shape. She hadn't had sex in mind. She wanted to talk. He'd hoped that she'd been longing as much as him. She took his hand and they went down to the jetty. She babbled on about the summer party. She rejected all his intimate attempts. His hand cupped her soft perfect breast. He whispered in her ear how much he loved her. How much he wanted her. He'd got hard as soon as the car was gone. But she wriggled away. He saw her disappear into the cottage.

I will always miss you!

As long as I'm not whole I will miss you!

Who would I be if I started to dance with life?
If life in its whole was an expression of
a complete woman.
If the imprint and the expression was a dream as
much in me as around me.
If this whole couldn't be separated:
Who am I then?

The couples therapist Ann sleaplessly continues her life in a shapeless haze. Her divorce uproots her usually safe and comfortable life. She's heading towards something new, but her confusion paralyses her. Her roots seem to go back in time. Even further back than she would ever have emagined.
Does this have anything to do with her incomprehensible dreams?

She tries to sort out her life and inner turmoil. The separation throws her into a precipice, at the same time she sees her closest friend enjoying different men. Then Mia enters with other perspectives and turns Ann's whole world of perception upside-down.

Who is she really beneath all these ingrained opinions?

Who is she, the woman who is free to dance with life?

I am grateful for this novel which celebrates the woman for what she has been and what she will become.

Christina Divèn, health coach.

A lovely book.
Women Dancing in Pine Valley
is incredebly timely!

Kristina Pannblom cert. TCM acupuncturist.

www.ingramcontent.com/pod-product-compliance
Lightning Source LLC
La Vergne TN
LVHW040000200726
843493LV00005B/1073